The Falling Away
Christian End Times Novel

By

Cliff Ball

Published by Cliff Ball
The Falling Away
Christian end times fiction
Book 1 of Perilous Times Series
Visit cliffball.net

ISBN-13: 978-1517757007
ISBN-10: 1517757002

Chapter 1

"Okay, now the next items on our list are incoming patients. The first patient is a man named Will Carson, age seventy-five. According to the paperwork, he came down with a severe case of pneumonia after a double bypass and had to go on a ventilator because he was getting too weak to breathe on his own. The small-town hospital who had him previously thinks he doesn't have much longer to live, so they sent him to our ICU. As with other cases like these, we'll make him as comfortable as we can, but we'll not go above and beyond. Are we in agreement, Doctor Kirkland?" asked Gina Dodd, the government overseer for this hospital.

Doctor Neal Kirkland spent another moment wishing he had retired when the federal government took over the healthcare system over a decade ago, but he liked the money he made and didn't want to give it up. He continued to wonder if other government overseers at other hospitals were as cold and black-hearted as Dodd was towards dying patients. When she was lit a certain way, she sort of reminded him of the wicked witch in the old Disney cartoon

Snow White. Kirkland thought that for a forty-five year old, she looked decades older than she was, and looked used up, probably from all the nicotine and alcohol she'd consumed over the years.

As for himself, although he was a little older than Dodd, many people assumed he was in his late twenties to mid-thirties, which was both an insult and compliment depending on his mood at the time. He figured that he didn't look his age because it was either from his good genetics or because he was a teetotaler. Not that it mattered all that much to him. His job was now his life since his wife died a few years ago and his adult children were scattered across the country living their lives.

From what Kirkland could observe of Dodd, she seemed to enjoy telling families that the government was not going to spend the money to keep their loved ones alive, even if that loved one was the breadwinner of the family. It was a shame really; decades ago a person could survive a quadruple bypass and be none the worse for wear, but now….

"Doctor Kirkland, can you get your head out of the clouds and care to join me and the rest of your staff in this important discussion that we have every single day?"

Kirkland looked at the obviously irritated Dodd, who was tapping her fingers on the table. He replied, “Sorry, my mind wandered. Uh, we’ll definitely make Mr. Carson as comfortable as we can. I do have a question though, if I may?”

Scowling, Dodd asked, “What is it?”

“I know a man his age rarely ever survives the kind of pneumonia he has, but what-if Mr. Carson pulls through? We’d have to get him a bed in the recovery wing, so does he have the kind of insurance that’ll allow him to stay?”

“Well, if the impossible happens, Mr. Carson is a retired government employee, meaning he has the best insurance in the land. So, we’ll drain his medical account dry until we’re required to release him, simple as that,”

“I see. Are you going to talk with the family about accepting Mr. Carson’s eventual death?”

“Of course. Let me see what their religious preferences are and I’ll talk to them about preparing for his death.” Dodd shuffled through the paperwork and found what she needed. “Ah, here it is. According to the previous hospital, his wife basically spent twenty-four hours a day by her husband’s side, watching his vitals like a hawk. Well, she won’t be able to spend the night here, so she won't interfere nearly as much. Anyway, they're Christians, apparently from a much stricter denomination than most we encounter. I'll tell them I'm a chaplain and if they need me, I'll be around, even though I won't be,"

"Don't you think they'll see through that? Do you even know if they accept women chaplains?"

"Honestly, I don't care. Just do your job, Doctor, and the same goes for you nurses. Got it?" The nurses around the conference table acknowledged the order. "Okay, who are these other patients we need to discuss?"

Hours later, Doctor Kirkland came into the private room of Will Carson. Carson was on a ventilator, deep asleep, probably from all the drugs pumped through the IV's, and he looked like he was on the edge of death. His skin was very pale, almost translucent, and he had apparently lost a lot of weight. Carson's wife, Laura, was sitting by the bed, with her eyes closed and holding on to her husband's hand. Neal cleared his throat and Laura looked up at him with red-rimmed puffy eyes, giving Neal the impression that she'd been crying for hours.

"I'm sorry to interrupt, but I'm Doctor Neal Kirkland, head of the ICU at this hospital. You must be Mr. Carson's wife, Laura,"

"Uh, yes, I am." Laura got up from her chair, approached Doctor Kirkland, and offered to shake his hand, which he did. "How do you think he's doing?"

"Well, right now, your husband is not doing so well, but I hope that changes. We'll do what we can for him though,"

"Thank you, I appreciate the hard work you and your nurses are putting in to help my husband get better, and I hope God blesses you,"

"Thanks, I guess. All right, I'll check his vitals and if any of his IV's need replacing, I'll send the nurse in. Remember Mrs. Carson, you need to take care of yourself. Do you have any children that can help?"

"Yes, my sons and their wives are on their way, they'll be here in a day or two, since they live in other states. Do you have any idea when my husband might get out of ICU?"

"I really don't know at the moment, Ms. Carson, but we'll do what we can for him, and we'll see in a week or two how well he's doing. I'll go ahead and check his vitals and then I'll leave you alone." Kirkland listened to Will Carson's heart and lungs, and what he heard wasn't encouraging. He hoped the Carson family was prepared for their patriarch's death. A few minutes later, he left the room to visit with other patients.

Laura could tell that Doctor Kirkland was worried, so she prayed, “Heavenly Father, please continue to watch over my husband and please continue to heal him. I pray for Doctor Kirkland’s ability to help restore my husband’s health and if he doesn’t know you as his Lord and Savior, I ask that you help me lead him to you. In your name, I pray, amen.”

A few hours later, Gina Dodd came into the Carson room prepared to act like one of the hospital chaplains. This time, Laura was reading from what looked like an e-reader while sitting at her husband’s bedside. Dodd cleared her throat, Laura looked up, and Dodd said, “Hi, I’m one of the hospital chaplain’s, Gina Dodd, do you need someone to talk or to minister to you?”

Laura thought she could sense some kind of evil presence around Dodd, which gave her the shivers, but she ignored it, and replied, “Thanks, but I have a pastor, and he’s coming tomorrow,”

“I just thought you might want to discuss your husband’s possible death and what you can do to prepare, since the government tends to be very stingy when it comes to matters like this,”

“I don’t believe Will is dying, because if he was dying, God would give me peace about his going home to be with Christ. I don't feel peace about being without him, so I know he's not going to die,"

Dodd wanted to roll her eyes, thinking, *Man, this woman's crazy for believing that, but I guess she has to cope some way.* Out loud, she replied, "I'm sure God will do what you need, but are you prepared to face your husband's death in case it does happen and the bills that follow?"

Laura felt her ire rising, so she asked God to help her to be calm with this so-called chaplain. "Miss Dodd, I am prepared, including being prepared for the inevitable bills that'll come, but as I said, my husband will get well. I appreciate your concern, but I really don't have need of your services. Thank you for visiting."

The nerve of this woman to dismiss me like that. Well, I tried, whatever happens is her fault. Dodd thought. "Okay, well, I wish you the best, Mrs. Carson. Goodbye." The two women shook hands and Dodd left the room.

A few days later, Doctor Kirkland returned to the Carson room to find the family praying around the older Carson's bed, alongside a man around Kirkland's age the doctor wasn't familiar with. Even though he was skeptical of prayer, Kirkland decided to wait before he interrupted the family. He patiently listened as Laura, her two sons, their wives, and the pastor prayed for Will Carson. He hoped praying gave the family some peace, since last Kirkland had heard, Mr. Carson was still critical, but wasn't better or worse.

"Our God in Heaven, we come to you to ask that you intercede on Will's behalf. We ask that you restore Will's health to what it once was and that he maintains good health for many more years. I pray for Laura's health as she deals with this, and please give her the strength and wisdom to help her husband recover later on. I thank you for their children, who have been a great help to their parents, and you reward them as you see fit. Thank you for the doctors, the nurses, and everyone who works in this hospital, please help them to have the knowledge to heal Will. In everything we do, we give thanks to you, Lord. In Jesus' name we pray, amen." Prayed the man who Kirkland didn't know.

The family all said amen, and that gave Kirkland the opening to say, "Hi, I'm sorry to interrupt, I just came over to check on the patient." Kirkland walked up to the man who just prayed, extended his hand for a handshake, and asked, "I haven't met you yet, I'm their doctor, Neal Kirkland,"

"Hi, Doc, I'm their pastor, Sam Rogers," Rogers replied as he shook Kirkland's hand.

"How's he doing today, Mrs. Carson?" Kirkland had the latest vitals on his tablet, but thought it was better to show the family that he cared about Mr. Carson.

"I think he's getting better, he actually opened his eyes twenty or so minutes ago, and even squeezed my hand. How great is that?" replied Laura.

Kirkland didn't expect to hear that, and asked, "Even though he's on a ventilator, did he try to say anything?"

"No, he seemed really groggy, but I told him everything would be all right and that we're praying for him. He went back to sleep right after,"

"Well, being groggy is expected. I'm glad he's beginning to respond to our care. Did you inform the nurses when that happened? They might be able to provide better care if they know he's beginning to respond to it,"

"I would, but they ignore me when they don't act like I'm annoying them, and they usually tell me to go home,"

"I'll speak to them about their attitudes towards a patient's family, especially yours. Okay, I'll go ahead and check his heart rate and lungs,"

Kirkland listened to Will's heart, which sounded much stronger than the last time he heard it earlier in the week. Meanwhile, the rumbling in the lungs from the pneumonia sounded like there was less fluid on the lungs, giving the doctor some hope that Will was on the mend. Standing up straight after using the stethoscope, Kirkland looked at the Carson family, and saw that they were hoping to hear good news, so he said, "His heart sounds stronger and I think his pneumonia is starting to clear up, I'll have an X-Ray ordered for him so we can find out for sure. All in all, it looks like things are looking up."

"Oh, thank God!" exclaimed Laura, as her sons and daughters-in-law started hugging her. "Thank you, Doctor Kirkland, for helping him to get better,"

"You're very welcome. If there's anything else I can do, don't hesitate to ask. I have to check on my other patients, so I'll see all of you later."

They bid him goodbye and as he walked away, Kirkland wondered about their beliefs in God. He never denied there was a God, he just hadn't thought about a higher power than him since he was a child, as his family were far from the church-going types, maybe visiting a church around Christmas or Easter. The church his family visited was usually the type that put on a stage show, but the pastor never preached anything that would make anyone mad or uncomfortable.

It was obvious to Kirkland that prayer worked for the Carson family, since the elder Mr. Carson was getting better in spite of people like Dodd not wanting to do their best to help the sick get healthy again. Kirkland made a mental note to ask the Carson's about their faith and belief in God when he had the time. Meanwhile, he had fifty patients to check up on and there were only so many hours in a day.

Chapter 2

Across the country at a private lab, a group of scientists worked on various ways to transmit lethal viruses, including manipulating the genetic codes of those viruses so the viruses could be even more lethal than they already were. One engineer/scientist, Steve Thacker, came up with an idea, so he went to his boss, John Warren. Once he was in Warren's office, the scientist told him. "Mr. Warren, I think I know of a better way to have a transmittable virus that is nearly one hundred percent lethal,"

"What's your idea, Steve?"

"While I think genetically modifying viruses is a good idea, I propose we use nanotechnology to spread it quicker,"

"You mean we should use nanobots to spread the viruses?"

"Yes, sir. We could program a bunch of the little guys to make it look like the person infected has so-and-so virus, and the only way to cure the problem is to remove the nanobots, hack into their programming, or for someone to figure out how to short out the electronics. Since we and the government would be the only ones who know exactly what's happening, no one would be able to stop anyone from dying,"

"How would these nanobots spread?" John was genuinely interested in the idea and wanted to know more.

"First, they're programmed to replicate. Secondly, they'll also be programmed to infect other people, through contact or fluids. Sort of similar to how the Borg do it in *Star Trek*, but without all the extra tech required to physically interact with the other person to spread the bots. What do you think?"

"I think you have a great idea, Steve. Do you have any figures on how many would die in such a scenario?"

"Well, my simulations show that at least one-third of the world's population would die off if we unleashed the nanobots. In the real world, those figures could be either smaller or greater than the simulations conducted on my computer."

"Okay, that'll help when I speak with my superiors about this idea, so be ready with your presentation when the time comes for you to speak to them about it. Good job." John patted Steve on the shoulder, giving the scientist a smile as he escorted Steve out of the office.

Steve was relieved. He wasn't sure if his boss would take to the idea, but he did, and now all he had to do was wait for John to talk to the higher-ups. *If they approve of the initial idea, I wonder when I'll get to present the full idea for the project to them?* he wondered. In the meantime, Steve went back to his lab to conduct more simulated tests, while he hoped the higher-ups would allow him to conduct live tests on humans to see if his idea would work in the real world.

John closed the door, went back to his desk, and through email informed his superiors that he wanted to talk to them later in the day. Messages from each of them popped up within a few minutes of each other to inform him they would be ready for the conference call. John decided to conduct the teleconference after normal working hours so his secretary or any of the other employees wouldn't disturb the virtual meeting.

When he confirmed that his secretary, a majority of the lab techs, scientists, and normal workers were gone for the night, John activated the high definition screen used for conference calls. The people he reported to were scattered all over the planet, so getting them together in person usually proved difficult. The conference call was highly secure thanks to many algorithms that prevented hackers, ranging from private citizens to rogue countries, from intercepting the call and releasing the contents of the meeting to websites and news organizations.

As soon as their faces appeared, John began, "Ladies and gentlemen, thank you for taking time out of your busy day to join me. I called you to discuss an idea one of my scientists came up with in regards to the project. I have access to his files, so if you want to skip talking to him later, we can access the files and discuss the idea,"

"First of all, Warren, tell us the idea and if you think it's doable. If we think the idea should proceed, then we'll ask to speak to your scientist so we can hear what he has to say," replied Joseph Barker, the head of the World Health Organization.

"All right. The proposal was that we could use nanotechnology to spread fatal viruses faster or to simulate those viruses. Either way, it would still kill off anyone infected. He thinks at least one-third of the world's population would die off quickly,"

"Hmm.... sounds promising. Are you able to provide details on how he plans on preventing these tiny robots, if that's what they are, from targeting people like us?" asked Victor Shultz, the head of the biggest bank on Earth.

"He didn't say and I didn't think to ask. He mostly told me that the bots could replicate, but he wasn't sure if his simulations of the effects would be larger or smaller in the real world. I'm sorry I can't provide any more information, but I could access his files right now,"

"That's not necessary, John. We would prefer to speak to your scientist ourselves. However, the information you've provided with us so far is intriguing, although I'm a bit skeptical. When can we speak with him?" asked Barker.

"Today is Thursday, so how about Monday? I'll tell him tomorrow, which will give him the weekend to prepare a presentation of his idea,"

John's superiors cut the sound so he couldn't hear them talk among themselves for a few minutes. Resisting the urge to start tapping his fingers on his desk, because he was always impatient, he silently waited for them to finish their discussion. He didn't have to wait long.

"Okay, John, we'll wait until Monday to hear what your scientist has to say. We want you to ask him to prepare a cost analysis of the project, how the robots will be able to distinguish between the rabble and the elite, if he has a sample group he'd like to experiment on first, and if he thinks the robots will stop when the goal of one-third of the population is reached. Do you have any concerns of your own?"

"No, sir. I'll let my scientist know what you want and we'll talk again on Monday."

"We'll be waiting." Barker replied and then the screen went dark, which told John that they finished talking to him.

The next day, John informed Steve he'd have to speak with the higher-ups and what would be required of him. Steve really wasn't thrilled with working over the weekend to put everything together, but he did want to be recognized as someone who the elites of the world could rely on, so he didn't complain. Luckily, he had a lab at home he could use to work on his presentation for Monday. Having that lab at home was considered illegal by the United States government and could get him into trouble if anyone found out, especially if the bad guys got a hold of his experiments by hacking his computer. Steve thought something like that wouldn't happen and never put a thought into such a scenario occurring.

On Monday, Steve was nervous, but prepared for his presentation. He walked into the conference room expecting to speak with the higher-ups in person, but instead, he found them being holographically projected into the room. *I didn't know we had that kind of technology. Cool!* Steve thought as he sat down. He also thought it was lucky that most of his presentation was on his thumb drive, so he could send his presentation virtually and they'd be able to read it on their own devices.

"All right, Steve, are you ready to present your idea?" asked John.

"Yes, sir. I'll send the details to your various devices so you'll be able to follow along." Steve inserted the thumb drive into the digital projector, which also had the ability to transmit data to other devices since it connected to the lab's wireless network. When the presentation loaded, he asked, "Has everyone received the data?"

Everyone indicated they had, so he began, "As we know, transmitting viruses is a complicated matter and tends to be random. We usually don't know if the modified virus will infect as many people as we'd like or if it'll burn itself out before it has a chance to spread to a wide enough population to be self-sustaining. For example, Ebola showed us the difficulty in controlling a naturally occurring virus. However, if we use nanotechnology, we can control how long the virus will last, where it spreads to, and who it spreads to. The programming language is simple, so anyone can control how, when, and where the bots will initiate the virus. The bots are also programmed to replicate, so the cost will be minimal, since all one has to do is build four or five, and they'll construct more as they infect a body. Once a point has been reached where an infected body has enough bots to accomplish its mission, they'll begin searching out other hosts through various means, such as adapting into an airborne virus to search for more victims,"

"Excuse me, Doctor Thacker, I have a question for you," interrupted Charles Morris, richest man in the United States, the creator of the most used operating system for computers, and self-proclaimed humanitarian.

"Go ahead, sir,"

"I'm familiar with the idea of using nanotech to simulate viruses and spread them, since I've experimented with the idea myself, so what makes yours different?"

"Well, to be blunt, sir, my nanobots will use an operating system that I created from scratch. I read about your experiments before I tried it myself, but I realized it wouldn't work with your operating system. Your OS is designed to be buggy so you'll have customers that will keep buying the next update. Your engineers were shortsighted when it came to using the OS for your nanotech and they didn't think to create a new operating system, so your company's attempt was doomed to fail,"

"I see. I'd say that was very forward thinking of you, Thacker. I'll have to speak with my engineers about creating a more stable OS in future tech that only the government buys for situations such as the one we're discussing. Thank you for answering the question."

"Mr. Thacker, even though you say the bots will be cheap to produce, I don't see anywhere in your proposal the actual cost of the initial production. Do you have a ballpark figure or are we to begin constructing the tech just on your say so and not worry about the cost?" asked Victor Shultz.

"Sorry about that, Mr. Shultz, I didn't include it because I didn't think the cost was that high. Well, the cost I came up with, after conducting many simulations, is less than five million dollars,"

"Really? I'll have to say I'm a bit surprised by such a low figure. Would you care to explain why you think that's all that it'll cost?"

"Since I only have to construct about five to start off with, they'll cost one million dollars each. After that, the bots will take care of the rest,"

"I see. I believe my bank can afford to fund your experiment, as long as it remains as low as you think it will and there's no project creep and cost override. You'll get your money, Mr. Thacker,"

"Thank you, Mr. Shultz,"

"Mr. Thacker, where do you propose we should release the first batch of these nanobots?" asked Morris.

"I think where all of the artificial viruses are always released before they go world-wide – Africa. A country like Liberia always seems to be a good place for ground zero, so that's where we should start,"

"I think that's a great idea. How would you prevent these bots from infecting the wrong people?"

"I'll program into the bots the information about who and who not to target, probably though specific DNA markers,"

"Excellent. Can you program the nanobots to replicate any disease?"

"Yes, sir. Were you thinking of Ebola, or perhaps something more virulent?"

"No, Ebola is what I was thinking of, since it's one of the worst. This kind of thing will reduce the population of our planet to a more reasonable level and those left will be much easier to control. Other means of reducing the population have shown not to work as well as reported when I first invested in those projects, like sterilization through Polio or Measles shots. I have one last question, Mr. Thacker. How do we know this information will be kept quiet and will not blow up in our faces?"

"All of the information about the nanobots and this project are kept in a secure database unconnected to the internet so hackers will have no way of getting the data. We have the media on our side, so if someone does try to blow the whistle later on, there'll be no one reporting on it. If someone does figure out that the virus is artificial, we have people who will take care of that problem,"

"Excellent. I believe I'm convinced this project is worth pursuing and I'm sure my colleagues are also convinced. When can you launch them, Mr. Thacker?"

"I believe within the next two months, sir."

"I'm sure we all look forward to that day of the launch. Thank you for your time, Mr. Thacker. You'll have your money and the resources to finish your project within the day. You're free to go back to work." replied Joseph Barker.

"I appreciate the time you took out of your busy day to listen to me. Good day." Thacker left the room and went back to work. The higher-ups ended their conference a short time later, after discussing what to do with Thacker and his team once the project took a life of its own.

Chapter 3

"Today, the new Pope, who has been given the name, Peter, is expected to make his first appearance after being elected to the position last night. His biography says that he's from the Eastern Orthodox sect of the church, was born in Istanbul, and for a Pope, he is a very young man, being only thirty years of age. According to the press release from the Church, he believes that everyone worships the same god, there are many ways to get to heaven, and he would like the world's religions to cast aside their differences and come together as one people. He believes in man-made climate change, that capitalism is sinful, and believes the world is over-populated.

"There's a loud minority from different sects who claim that he's the last Pope, the one who will usher in some type of apocalyptic era that will destroy Earth and all the supposedly evil people inhabiting our planet. The Church says that these people don't have any idea what they're talking about, are delusional, and will be dealt with when the time comes to deal with such people." The reporter paused for a moment, apparently listening to someone talking to him over his earpiece. “All right, we’ve been told the Pope is about to step out onto the balcony to speak. We now go live to the Vatican.”

The scene switched to a camera focused on St. Peter’s Square. The camera showed the thousands of people gathered so they could listen to the new Pope in person, then it slowly made its way across the Square to focus on the balcony that Pope Peter would be appearing from. A few minutes later, curtains opened to reveal the Pope coming outside and then he stood on the balcony, waving to those gathered. As the reporter said, the Pope was very young compared to his predecessors and he definitely looked like he was from Turkey.

Even though Peter could speak in his native tongue, he began his speech in Italian, “Good day, my friends, my brothers and sisters. I’m glad to be here today, sharing with you my new journey as the new Pope of Rome. This journey of ours will be full of love, hope, and friendship, which no one can tear asunder.

“Let us always pray for one another, pray for a spirit of friendship among all the people of the world, and pray for those poor, misguided souls out there that will not join us in friendship because they do not have the same heart full of hope and love that we do.

Pray that Our Lord and Lady will forgive them of their sins so that they may join the rest of us in this new spirit of cooperation we will have. Now I bless the people of the world who have good will, and hope it will forever permeate our world.

"Brothers and sisters, I have to leave you now. Thank you for your welcome. Continue to pray for me until we meet again. We will see each other soon. Later today, I will pray to Our Lady, that she may watch over all of Rome. Good day to you all!" Peter left the balcony, accompanied by his staff.

Once inside, he spoke with his advisors, "First, we need to reach out to heads of the other religions so we can come together for a meeting of the minds. Such a meeting would probably take a few months to setup. Secondly, what can we do about the people who refuse to join us in the spirit of love, hope, and friendship?"

"We can start by dismissing them as a fringe of lunatics who can't see that bringing the religions of the world together is the right thing to do, since doing so will bring about love and friendship among all humans. We keep the pressure up and eventually these malcontents will be considered the enemy of peace and they must be sought out and destroyed. Would this please you, Your Most Holy?"

"I think what you suggest is a great idea. Our friends in the Middle East have killed many of the ones who think Rome does not speak for our holy one, but we still have problems with these small groups of malcontents in parts of Europe and the Americas. I also think we ought to encourage the world governments to come together to join us in love and friendship. It may take time for these ideas to come together, but I think we can do it. Now, my friends, let us pray."

Unbeknownst to everyone but the top echelons of the Catholic Church and those in power over various countries, Peter and his top Cardinals were not who they said they were. When Peter spoke of "Our Lord," he didn't mean Jesus, but of someone else, someone who was not yet ready to be revealed to the world. Men like Peter were put into place long ago to help bring an end to one religion being dominant over the others, especially in certain countries, and so that a one world religion, like a one world government, would hold sway over the people of Earth. For those in power, like Peter, it was about control over the people and by any means necessary.

Meanwhile, Doctor Kirkland found the Carson family watching the coverage about Pope Peter, mostly because it seemed to be on every channel. Will Carson was still weak, but he was doing much better, and was able to talk to his family for short periods before his medication caused him to fall asleep. Laura was shaking her head at the coverage, so Kirkland asked, "What do you think of this new pope?"

"Well, my family doesn't believe he or his church speaks for God. We believe we can go to God ourselves and speak to Him without an intermediary. My family and I, along with a group of people we associate with, believe that Jesus died for our sins, rose again three days later after paying for those sins, and will come back for us soon. Let me ask you something, Doctor. Do you know where you'll go when you die?"

To himself, Kirkland thought, *Man, this family is unusual, I don't think I know of anyone who believes in much of anything when it comes to a deity. I wonder why they do?* Then he said, "I don't know, to Heaven, I guess. I hadn't really thought about it,"

"Why do you think you'll go to Heaven?"

Shrugging, he replied, "I guess because I've tried to do good for others and I've given back to my community,"

"I'm afraid just being a good person and giving back won't get you there. If that was all that was required to go to Heaven, then every Tom, Dick, and Harry who did a tiny bit of good in their lives would also get there, even if they were mass murderers. If nearly everyone went to Heaven, then we might as well still live on Earth if we're going to be immortal. Heaven would be a pointless place, as Hell would be, if no one was rewarded for following God completely, or no one punished for not following God at all, especially if they kept rejecting Him. Would you like to know how you could assured that you would go to heaven when you die?"

"Sure, I guess,"

"Great. In order to go to Heaven, it's required that you accept that Jesus died for your sins and you're a sinner. That you accept He rose again on the third day after his crucifixion to show he was the Messiah and He lived a sinless life so He could pay for your sins. You need to accept that He's the only begotten son of God and you need to understand that only He can forgive you of all of your sins since you can't save yourself. I don't have my Bible with me, so I can't show you the verses, but I can give you a tract that explains all of this, if you want it,"

Skeptical, but intrigued, Kirkland said, "All right, I'll take it. Is there a way I can contact you or your church if I have even more questions?"

"You bet there is. The address and phone number for where we meet is on the back of the tract, so if you want to visit on a Sunday morning, we meet at 11 a.m. Pastor Rogers can even give you some of his time if you do have lots of questions. Okay?" Laura reached into her purse, pulled out the tract, and handed it to Kirkland.

"Okay." He took the tract Laura handed to him. "Thanks." Kirkland glanced at it, saw that it was a very short brochure type thing, and figured he'd look at it when he was at home.

"No problem, Doctor. So, how's Will doing?"

"I think he's doing far better than expected. His vitals are stronger and I believe we can let him go near the end of the month. I'm sure you'll be glad to get him home,"

"Oh, yes. I have a hard time sleeping in our bed without him there and I miss him terribly when he's not home with me. Thank you for helping him to get better,"

"You're very welcome, Mrs. Carson. I'd like to chat some more, but I have other patients to attend to. Have a great day."

"You too and I hope you have a blessed day."

Kirkland walked out of the room. His interest piqued by what Mrs. Carson was telling him when it came to Heaven and Christ dying for his sins. He thought about it until he was home, read the tract, and tried to do some research online to help with his decision, but most searches came up empty. It was mostly because the government had been purging Christian websites and the like from the internet, which was something Kirkland didn't know. He made a decision to visit the Carson's house of worship that Sunday.

On Sunday, he entered the address into Google Maps on his cell and the directions popped up on the screen. Kirkland noticed that the address was on the outskirts of town, but didn't give it much thought after that. Twenty minutes later, he found the address. He realized it was someone's private home, which looked sort of like a modernized version of the Cartwright home on the television series *Bonanza*. The home apparently sat on a couple of acres, surrounded by some kind of crops. There were about a dozen cars in the driveway, so he parked, got out of the car, and headed for the house.

At the door, Pastor Rogers and his wife greeted him, and the Pastor said, "Good morning, Doctor Kirkland. You haven't met my wife, have you?

"No, sir,"

"Doctor Kirkland, this is Erika. Erika, Doctor Kirkland was Will Carson's doctor when he was in the hospital,"

"I'm glad to meet you, Doctor,"

"I feel likewise, Mrs. Rogers," they shook hands.

"I'm honored that you decided to visit us this morning. Laura Carson mentioned that you might," replied Pastor Rogers.

"I'm curious about your beliefs and I wanted to know more,"

"Well, you've come to the right place. Come on in and find yourself a chair,"

"Okay." Before going inside, Kirkland asked, "Can I ask something?"

"I'll do my best to answer your question, Doctor,"

"How come your church is meeting here? I thought you would've been meeting in a building dedicated for that sort of thing,"

"Normally, we would be in a church building, but these are not normal times. Suffice it to say, the church in general is undergoing tremendous persecution in this day and age, and most of us can no longer meet in the buildings. So, we've decided to meet in individual homes. If you have time later, I'll tell you why we're doing this, all right?"

"All right and thank you for letting me visit your church."

"You're very welcome." Rogers and Kirkland shook hands, then the doctor went to sit down, and waited for the services to begin.

Kirkland noticed there were fifty people meeting here today and luckily, the house was more than big enough to accommodate that many people. Thanks to Pastor Rogers, Mrs. Rogers, and Laura Carson, he was able to meet every person attending the meeting, and they were all very nice to him. The service began with singing and fifteen minutes later Rogers was ready to start preaching. He preached on a passage in the book of Revelation about the Tribulation, including something about a recent Blood Moon, which was new to Kirkland, so it was above his head. Then Rogers said something that surprised the doctor.

"I believe the new pope is the false prophet as described by John in our text. Pope Peter believes all religions of this world ought to come together and thinks there are many ways to heaven. This false prophet will open the door for a man to come in and deceive the people of this world into eventually worshipping him. The leader will lead the world himself with no other governments in charge and will be known to us as the anti-Christ, because he'll declare he is the Christ. Now, many really don't know if the church will be raptured before the Tribulation or in the middle of it, so please be prepared for these two evil men when they show themselves for who they really are. Personally, I believe that the anti-Christ will show up after the church and its saints have been raptured. If you don't believe in Jesus Christ as your savior, then this is the perfect time to accept Him into your heart so you'll have the discernment to see what's happening. Now, let's pray as I end the service."

Kirkland watched some of the congregation go up front to a makeshift altar and pray. He had many questions, but decided to wait for the service was over with to ask the pastor about those questions. Kirkland approached Rogers, and said, "I'd like to talk with you a bit, if you have time,"

"I have time, this is my home, so I don't need to be anywhere at the moment. Can you stay for lunch? My wife will be done making it shortly,"

"Sure,"

"All right, I'll tell her to set an extra plate. I'll be right back." Rogers went to the kitchen and told his wife they would have an extra place at the table for the meal. When he returned, he asked, "What would you like to talk about?"

"Well, I'd like to ask about accepting Christ as my savior. The tract Mrs. Carson gave me makes it look like it's easy to do, but there's got to be more to it. Right?"

"Nope, that's all there is to getting saved. Christ didn't want to make it so complicated that it's confusing. You simply accept that He died for your sins, ask Him to forgive you of those sins, and then He'll save you through His grace,"

"But what if I stumble and sin more?"

"You won't lose your salvation, because Christ died once for us. If we lost our salvation, then Christ dying for our sins would've been pointless, since He would've had to come back multiple times to repeat what was done,"

"All right. Do I need to give back to my community, donate more to charity, and do other good works to be guaranteed to go to heaven?"

"No, none of that will help you get to Heaven, although doing so in the name of our Lord will help you have a greater reward when you get to heaven,"

"Okay, thank you for answering those questions. I think I'm ready now, what do I do now?"

"All you have to do is pray that Christ forgives you of your sins and then ask Him to save you from those sins so that you'll go to heaven when you die. Okay?"

"Got it," Kirkland closed his eyes to pray and did what Pastor Rogers told him to do to be saved. After doing so, Kirkland felt a burden lifted off his shoulders.

"Feel better?"

"Yes, and I feel different, like I'm a whole new person,"

"That's supposed to be how you feel. I'm glad I have a new brother in Christ. So, do you want to know anything else?"

"Yes, I have a couple other questions, like how come you no longer meet in a building?"

"For one, churches are no longer tax exempt, but we could've dealt with that, if that was the only reason. The other main reason is that the gays have been bullying and suing churches for not marrying them ever since the Supreme Court decision in 2015. That's in spite of most churches preferring to only marry their members, so most don't even do weddings at all these days. Some of these churches have been burned to the ground as a result, pastors imprisoned, and the membership sued beyond their capacity to pay the fine, so many church buildings have closed down as a result and sold off. Attendance is also down, since so few believe in Jesus these days, which is called a falling away. Then, there's the FCC taking down websites owned by churches, Christian businesses, and faith based blogs, which severely hampers our ability to reach out to the unsaved. They're attempting to make Christians disappear altogether, but our sects have survived for thousands of years under the Roman church's nose, and we can do it again,"

"I didn't know that. I'm sorry that's happening,"

"Me too, but it's all in God's plan and we win in the end,"

"You mean the whole end times prophecy thing you talked about earlier?"

"Yes, exactly,"

"How can I learn more about the end times?"

"Well, besides reading Revelation, I can give you study books from various sources that'll break down Revelation into more understandable language. Would you like that?"

"Yes, sir, I'd appreciate it if you did that. Thank you,"

"You're very welcome, Doctor,"

Mrs. Rogers came out of the kitchen, and said, "Lunch is ready, come and eat."

"Good, I'm starving. Come on, Doctor, let's eat."

The Rogers' and Kirkland talked about end times prophecy for the rest of the day. When Kirkland went home, he was happy with his decision to accept Christ and was brimming with excitement over his newfound knowledge that he hoped would help him understand what was going on in current events.

Chapter 4

Tim Richman was fed up with everything. Fed up with the government actively encouraging people to come to the United States illegally, fed up with them not assimilating, fed up with a small minority of the population getting their way through bullying, and fed up with everyone claiming white men had extra privileges and were the enemy of everyone else. While there were plenty of other things to be worried about, such as ISIS terrorist attacks that continued to increase each year, especially in the United States, Tim was obsessed with what angered and affected him personally. The straw that broke the camels' back for him was being fired from his job so he could be replaced by a non-English speaking illegal who had no business doing his job. However, a quota must be fulfilled at all costs, because the federal government would fine his former company thousands of dollars a day for not filling that quota.

At home the day he was fired, he complained to his wife, "Donna, I'm sick and tired of all of these people coming to our country illegally. I'm sick and tired of our government pitting people of different races against each other. I'm also sick and tired of the grievance mongers attacking American institutions because of some perceived wrongdoing in the past, and then claim that it all must be eliminated from our history. I'm tired of going into the post office or the store and not being able to speak with another person who continues to speak in their native language and doesn't even try to learn English. If all of them assimilated, I wouldn't have a problem, but they're not, so I do. I'm even sick of having to pay more every year for government healthcare that gets worse every year. Something needs to be done,"

"Like what? Our rights are ignored, so protesting will get you thrown in jail if you're not part of the official groups sanctioned by the government. Besides, where are you going to get access to bullets, since most forms of weapon and ammo have been banned?"

"I don't know, but I'll figure something out,"

"Tim, please take some time to calm down before you do something we'll both regret. Please?"

Tim wasn't sure he wanted to calm down, but since his wife asked him to, he only replied, "Oh, all right, but you know none of those issues will go away if we ignore them,"

"I know, but it would be nice if they did. Anyway, what do you want for supper?"

"Got any hamburgers?"

"Sure. Want all the fixings?"

"Of course."

"Okay, we'll eat in half an hour."

While his wife cooked dinner, Tim still thought about ways he could voice his displeasure without Donna knowing. Complaining online would do no good, most of his favorite opinion sites were now offline because of the FCC and their supposed fairness policy when it came to political opinions and the FBI would likely monitor his blog. Facebook and Twitter were a no-go, since he'd be banned instantly for having contrary ideas to the powers-that-be. Writing to the newspaper for an editorial would be ignored, but could get him a home visit from DHS if something he wrote was inflammatory towards the government since the media tended to be on the side of the government and would report such things. He thought, *I think I'll be able to find a solution tomorrow after a good night's sleep, I'm sure of it. There has to be a way to show that a lot of us are unhappy with the state of things, there just has to be.*

The next day, Tim decided to drive around the city so he could figure out what to do. He ended up driving through an older part of town that looked like it had separated from the United States and it seemed to him like he had crossed the southern border. He saw car lots with Mexican flags flying, signs written in Spanish advertising the cars, and even grocery stores in other foreign languages that only catered to the foreign born, among other businesses that were doing the same. It infuriated him that America was no longer a melting pot, but now made up of islands of various nations in American cities, so now the country was no longer unique. Tim came up with an idea, so he parked his car, and began taking pictures of each property. He did this so he could study the photos later on and come up with a plan without getting into trouble with the authorities because some of the properties had video cameras that would record wrongdoing. Once he was satisfied, Tim went home, uploaded the pictures to his computer, and studied them for several hours before he finally knew what he should do.

In the middle of the night, Tim returned to the area to do what he planned, but he would start out small for this first night. He made his way to a car lot, which only had about two dozen older cars, and he easily disabled the video cameras before doing anything else. Once he accomplished that, Tim took down the ten Mexican flags surrounding the property and ripped them to shreds. Next, he used black spray paint and painted over the signs that in Spanish said, "No Credit Check" and "Low Down Payments." With the baseball bat he brought with him, Tim smashed the windows of half of the cars, used his Bowie knife to slash tires, and then used the bat to smash the windows of the small office building. On the front door, Tim wrote a message with spray paint, "We don't want you here. Go back to Mexico!" Satisfied with his work, Tim returned to his car, which sat parked half a mile away, and went home. He hoped that his little message had gotten through to the surrounding foreign owned businesses.

On local news the next day, which Tim thought only reported half the story like they always seemed to do, "This morning, we have a report of major vandalism committed to a locally owned auto dealership. Cars were vandalized and the office windows were broken. As of now, the police have no leads, but our reporter did speak to the business owner a short time ago,"

The man being interviewed spoke no English, so the reporter translated for him, "I want no trouble. I'm only here to make a living, to help my fellow Mexicans buy used cars. In Mexico, the gangs would take most of my money, saying it was for protection. I thought this did not happen here in the Land of the Free."

That's what you get for thinking, moron. Tim thought to himself.

"Mr. Perez does vow to continue selling cars at his location. The police representative to the press has said that the FBI, DOJ, and Homeland Security might be called in to investigate to see if this is a hate crime and they also state that whoever did the vandalism would be prosecuted to the full extent of the law. You'll be able to follow the full story on our website, where you'll be able to leave a comment on what happened. Now, we give you a weather update from our meteorologist, Jaimie Sanchez…."

Tim turned off the television and pondered what to do next. *Should I continue my crusade tonight or wait for everything to cool down before going out again? What should I do? I guess I could check out the TV stations' website to see what others are saying. Yeah, that's a good idea.* So, Tim went into the room containing the desktop and logged on.

The link to the story was easy enough to find and he was surprised to find a few hundred comments already. The way the comments were going, Tim was surprised the station hadn't scrubbed them from their website yet and disabled the comments. Many of the comments said stuff like, "The owner of the dealership should either learn English or go back to where he came from."

Some comments were a variation of, "I'd love to volunteer to collect protection money from Mr. Perez so he can continue to do business without trouble."

Other comments supported the business owner, "I think he has a right to come to the states and do business here, away from the corruption of Mexico. So what if he is illegal? We all belong to the human race, a border should mean nothing."

Easy for all of them to talk, the internet is safe to spew stupid ideas because of its anonymous nature and they don't have to actually do anything to back up an opinion, Tim thought, *but I do agree with a lot of them. I'd like to leave a comment, say I'm the one who did it and why, but I'm pretty sure the FBI's monitoring the comments. I just need to figure out how to do that without them making a surprise visit to my neighborhood.*

Tim brainstormed for a while before coming up with an idea – he could use the local library, which had its own computers and internet access so the FBI would have a difficult time figuring out who used the computer. Getting into his car, Tim drove to the nearest branch and made his way inside. Before doing anything he went to the front desk, and asked the clerk, "Do I need a library card to use the computers?"

"No, sir, but you do need a guest pass. You can use one of our computer's for one hour, because it'll log you out automatically after that. If the library's not busy and there's no one waiting to use a computer, we can extend your time, if you ask us to."

"Okay, got it." The clerk handed him a guest pass. "Thanks."

As soon as he logged on, Tim brought up the station's website page to the story. The comments were still being generated and so far the station hadn't purged any undesirable comments. Taking a deep breath, Tim registered with a fake name and a throwaway email address, and then began typing his thoughts in the comment box, even though he thought his comment might be ignored in all the noise.

"I'm quite concerned about our nation and where it's headed. Are we going to be like ancient Rome and let the barbarians at our gates overwhelm us and then let them destroy everything we've worked so hard to maintain? Once upon a time, before the whiners, grievance mongers, communists, progressives, and others took over our country, immigrants had to prove they could contribute to our nation. Now, we have people who leech off of hard working Americans, who don't bother to learn our history, our culture, or bother to learn English. They don't want to be a part of the melting pot. If we natural born Americans deigned to enter their countries and demanded the same things they demand of our government, we'd be arrested, jailed, and probably deported, or worse. I say we must put a stop to this, by any means necessary. If these immigrants, legal or illegal, don't assimilate, then we should make sure they leave. Since I'm the one who tore up that Mexican's place of business, I'd like to ask all of you who agree to join me in showing them we mean business. – A Concerned Citizen." Tim stopped there and submitted the comment.

Tim logged off the computer, went back to the desk, handed the guest pass back to the clerk, and went home. Later on that evening, he tuned into the ten o'clock news to see if the story had any updates and it had. "According to the FBI and Homeland

Security, they are becoming increasingly aware of threats to non-American residents by people who are willing to commit acts of domestic terrorism. The agencies are asking citizens to tone down the rhetoric before people end up getting killed. They also say they're investigating the damage done to Jose Perez's business early this morning, and they think they have some leads. Mr. Perez says he'll keep doing business at that location and will not be intimidated. We'll keep you updated on this story as more information becomes available. In other news, a relatively new company, Sol System Mining, has announced they'll be sending up mining equipment with a manned rocket launch to the moon within the month. They are achieving something other privately owned space companies have only talked about….."

Tim turned off the television, not caring about the moon story, wishing he could torch the car lot, but he knew the FBI and Homeland Security would be watching and waiting for something like that to happen. Since Tim lived in a metropolis consisting of dozens of small cities within half an hour's drive from his home, he could always try somewhere else.

Before he could plan anything, his wife reacted to the news, "Isn't what happened to that man's car lot horrible? Who would do such a thing? You wouldn't know anything about it, would you, Tim?"

Acting surprised, he replied, "No, why would I?"

"Oh, probably because of a conversation we had the other day about our country being ruined by people who don't assimilate,"

"Well, that doesn't mean I did anything, but whoever did it, more power to him,"

"I'm just worried that I'll find you in jail one of these days because you ended up saying something to the wrong person. Please be careful, 'k?"

"I'll do my best."

His wife being worried didn't bother Tim all that much, he was convinced he was doing the right thing. It was obvious he couldn't show up in the part of town where he vandalized the car lot, so he decided to go to another part of the metropolitan area to find another foreign business where he could show them his displeasure. The next morning, he decided he would investigate possible locations before he would do anything.

While driving, Tim heard a breaking news story on the radio, "This morning, we learned that four men have been arrested for setting fire to the car lot that had only been vandalized a few days ago. The men claimed to know nothing about the earlier vandalizing, but said they decided to finish the job. The bond for these men has been set at one million dollars each and they'll go before a judge in a few days so they'll know when their trials will be. The fire department arrived too late to save the building on the property, and there were cars with smoke and fire damage. Mr. Perez continues to say he will do what he has to do to stay in business."

What a bunch of idiots. They should've known the government would be watching. Tim thought while driving to find another place of business to vandalize.

An hour later, Tim found what he was looking for - a strip mall. It was early in the day, so none of the businesses were open yet. Driving through the parking lot, he could see that none of them, in his opinion, were owned by English speaking people and all of the businesses were foreign owned since the signage for each business was in a different language. Seeing that cameras only covered the front of the various businesses, Tim went to the alley behind the strip mall, parked, got out, and took a gas can with him. He poured gas into trash bins, along the walls of the strip mall, and anything else he thought was flammable. Once he was satisfied he had enough gas on everything, Tim used a lighter to start the fire and watched the buildings burn.

He stood in place for a minute, until he realized he had to get out of there before the fire and police departments showed up, Tim got back into his car and happily drove away. He hoped this would light a metaphorical fire underneath his fellow citizens and they would begin to take back the United States from these foreign invaders. Unfortunately, for Tim, the consequences of his actions in the coming months would go far beyond what he envisioned.

Chapter 5

Steve Thacker and his team were finally finished with the production and testing of the nanobots after three months of work. The bots going airborne worked quite well and managed to make every animal in the lab sick within minutes of insertion. The enhanced viruses were one hundred percent fatal to the lab animals, some taking only minutes to die once the bots activated in their bodies, while other animals took longer to die due to experimenting on the capabilities of the bots. Thacker and his team deactivated the bots once they achieved the primary goal.

Thacker went to see his boss about their progress, "Mr. Warren, my team and I have finished the lab tests of the nanobots and I believe they're ready for release into the world,"

"That's great news. I'll inform my superiors we're ready. Let your team know that I think all of you did a great job and we won't forget it,"

"Thank you, sir. Is there anything else you require of me?"

"No, just take a well-deserved break. All right?"

"We'll do that."

"You're dismissed, Steve."

Warren went to the conference room and sent a message to his superiors that he needed to speak with them. He knew they got the message when the holographic projectors formed the holographic versions of his superiors. Charles Morris was the first to speak. "What's your news, John?"

"Thacker and his team have informed me that the nanobots are ready for release,"

"Excellent. We'll send a security team to take possession of the technology within the hour. I want you to send us all of their research through our secure server after you get rid of Thacker and his team. Think you can do that?"

"Yes, sir. Do you have any preferences on how I should get rid of them?"

"No, we just want them gone, doesn't matter how. Our reasoning is so we'll have no one informing the media or other busy bodies about this project and have it transmitted all over the news. Are my instructions clear?"

"Yes, sir, I'll get to it right away,"

"Good. If that's it, we're done here. Good day, Warren." The holographic images deactivated.

Warren waited until the security team showed up to take possession of the technology before deciding what to do with Thacker and the team. An hour later, security showed up like Morris said they would. Warren stepped into the lab with security behind him, all of whom were armed and looked ready to participate in a battle. Thacker and his team looked like they were cleaning up the lab, so the scientist felt somewhat annoyed by the interruption, "What's going on here?"

"My superiors have decided to take possession of the technology, so that's why these men are here,"

"I'm not so sure that's a good idea,"

"You have no choice in the matter, Steve." Warren turned to the security team, "The nanobots are stored in the cold storage room, but they don't need to stay cold to be viable. The rest of the equipment is scattered throughout this lab. I'll deal with the computers and all of the files stored on their hard-drives. Please be careful, otherwise, you'll find yourself infected with some sort of virus that currently doesn't have a cure,"

"We'll take care of it, Mr. Warren. Men, get to work."

"I object, our equipment is very sensitive and these guys don't have the slightest idea how to handle the bots." complained Thacker.

“Don’t worry, it’s no longer your responsibility.” Warren replied.

Thacker and his team stood by helplessly as their lab was basically taken apart and most everything carried away. When all the equipment was gone, he asked Warren, “What now?”

Warren wasn’t looking forward to what was about to happen next. He wasn’t bloodthirsty by nature, but in order for what was planned to be able to succeed, some people had to be eliminated. “I’m sorry, but you’re no longer useful to my superiors. There’s a reason why the security team is also equipped with weapons,”

With a nod from Warren, the security team opened fire on the scientists. Some of the scientists tried to run, most cowered where they were, and a handful tried to beg for mercy, but their cries were ignored. The massacre didn’t take too long and when it was over, the head of security asked, “Is there anything else you need us to take care of before we leave?”

“No, that’s it. Thank you. Now I just need to figure out how to deal with this mess.” Security left and Warren looked around the now bloody, formerly sterile lab wondering what he should do now.

Before taking care of the mess, all of the data stored on the computers had to be transmitted to the main database of his superiors. Warren went to the main computer of the lab, logged on, and discovered there was over five hundred terabytes of information. Luckily, the internet speed was the best available, so it would only take a few minutes to transmit the information. Warren logged on to the secure server and then transmitted all the information about the project, and the transfer only took ten minutes.

After logging off the computer, he finally had an idea on how to deal with the mess. In other parts of the building, some scientists were experimenting with explosives that might be used on the surface of the moon or Mars for mining, so Warren thought a lab explosion would take care of his problem. Since there were still others in the building, he closed off Thacker's lab so no one would mistakenly go inside and find out what happened. He waited until quitting time before he retrieved the explosives, but he wasn't quite sure how much he needed.

The explosives were placed around the lab and Warren set a timer for fifteen minutes so he could be far enough away in case something calamitous happened to the whole building. If something that big occurred, he didn't worry about it because insurance would cover all the costs of whatever damage occurred. Warren briefly thought that maybe they could even blame the explosion on those people who were burning down minority owned businesses. However, his superiors and everyone else would probably be highly annoyed by the setback if other projects were destroyed, but Warren didn't know what else to do. He made his way to the parking lot, which was far enough away from the building, and waited for the explosion.

Ten minutes later, the explosives went off, causing a much bigger explosion than Warren had anticipated. Not only was Thacker's lab destroyed, but so was about half of the building, since other labs contained material that could easily enhance an explosive device. *They'll have my head!* Warren thought to himself, shocked by the magnitude of the explosion. *I had better get out of here before the cops and fire department shows up. Maybe my superiors will understand. I hope.* Warren found his car and was about to get inside it when he heard sirens in the distance. Stepping on the accelerator, he drove his car out of the parking lot as fast as it was able to go, fully aware that he needed to focus on driving so he wouldn't wreck the car and then get caught by the authorities.

At home, even though he didn't have access to a holographic projector or owned a webcam, Warren immediately called Morris on his phone. "Hello?" asked Morris.

"Mr. Morris, this is John Warren. I took care of the problem you asked me to take care of, but we know have an even bigger problem. One might say it was unintended consequences,"

"Is that why you're calling me from your unsecured home phone?"

"Yes, sir,"

"All right, since this call is unsecured, do your best to tell me what happened,"

"After taking care of the smaller problem, I decided to clean it up using some material of the unstable variety that our other employees were working on. Well, the material destroyed a good portion of the building and the rest caught on fire. I had to leave when I heard the fire department vehicles,"

Sighing, Morris replied, "That's unfortunate, but it's not entirely unexpected. Luckily, most of the experiments are being worked on in other locations in case we needed a backup plan. As for the building, we can blame it on domestic terrorism, which will be easy, since a lot of that is occurring lately. Don't you worry, John, we'll have everything taken care of, including you. Okay?"

"Okay. Thank you, sir,"

"You're welcome. I must go, because my wife is calling me to dinner. Goodnight, John." Morris hung up.

Later that night, Warren was asleep when he heard a noise loud enough to wake him up, so he got out of bed to investigate. Steeping into his living room, he was greeted by lights in his eyes from flashlights, and someone asking, "Are you John Warren?"

"Yeah. Who are you?"

"No one you need to worry about. You're coming with us."

The men grabbed Warren, a hood was pulled over his head, and they took him to a van, where he ended up shackled to a bench. No one said a word to him while they drove to wherever they were going and this situation frightened him. He wondered if his superiors were about to punish him for destroying their building, along with most of the experiments in the building. He decided it wouldn't be long before he found out.

The van stopped and Warren had no idea where. He remained shackled and the hood stayed over his head and face. He could barely hear someone outside of the van talking, but had no idea what they were saying, since the voices sounded muffled.

"Doctor Barker, are we ready for implantation?" asked Morris.

"Yes. The bots will remain deactivated until he lands in Liberia. From there, we'll activate them, and he'll be patient zero. If our estimates are right, the population of our planet should decline to below one billion within three years,"

"Excellent. Although, I think we should change the location where we drop him off, like in the middle of a large American city,"

"Why?"

"You've seen the news about the foreign businesses being burned down by some whites and then non-whites doing the same to white business. Because of that, the country seems to be on the verge of a race war. What better way to bring about the downfall of the United States than to have a white guy infect everyone with a virus that has no known cure and the very idea will cause everyone to lose their minds. What do you think?"

Barker thought about it for a moment, "I think that's a great idea. Many Americans travel overseas quite frequently, so the nanobots should be able to spread like wildfire. What city do you have in mind?"

"I think Oklahoma City would be a great city to implement our plan. It has four main highways going through it, along with railroads and a major airport. So with goods always going through there via freight truck and railroad car, the bots will spread quickly, along with help from everyday travel by our fellow humans via car and airplane. We need to place Warren in a good location, where there are lots of people,"

"Do you have any ideas, Mr. Morris?"

"I was thinking of a college football game, perhaps when the Sooners are playing at home,"

"That seems like a good idea. But, before we do that, should we knock him out before the shot is administered?"

"Yes,"

"All right, sounds like we have a plan. I'll administer the knockout drug before injecting him with the nanobots. I'll program the nanobots not to start infecting Warren until we're ready to start the outbreak. Are you going to address the media about the building being destroyed?"

"I'm about to do that, I just have to inform them first that I plan on addressing them." Morris sent a text message to his contacts in the press and each of them said they'd send a camera. Ten minutes later, remotely piloted camera drones showed up to film what Morris had to say. The drones were also equipped with microphones so a journalist could interview a person remotely without needing to be there in person for press conferences. For the press companies, drones were cheaper to use than paying to fuel up one of their company cars and for their employees to drive all over the place for their stories.

"Mr. Morris, we're ready to record whenever you're ready," stated a disembodied voice from one of the drones.

"All right and I want to thank the media companies for sending your various representatives. Last night, my lab came under attack and a good portion of the building ended up destroyed. Right now, we don't know if it was an ISIS terrorist attack or an attack by domestic terrorists. However, we do know that about two dozen of my scientists and engineers ended up killed in the attack. I've already sent the names of the people killed to your emails. I am offering a two million dollar reward for information on who did it and I'm asking that the individuals responsible be prosecuted to the full extent of the law. Okay, any questions?"

Since it was difficult to have multiple journalists back at their desk ask questions all at once using drones, Morris had a display on a tablet that informed him of who wanted to ask him something. He chose the first questioner, Dan Hill of the Global Cable Network, who asked, "Can you tell us what your people were working on?"

"I believe this particular lab was working on genetic therapies, the kind that would extend people's lifespans past one-hundred and twenty years, by at least twenty or thirty years,"

"Do you think religious fanatics from the Christian right might've objected to DNA experiments and took matters into their own hands, which is sort of similar to that whole controversy with that abortion provider a few years back?" asked Deanna Rowlett of the *New York Times*.

"Honestly, such a revelation wouldn't surprise me. Those particular Christians are in the way of progress and they must get out of the way voluntarily, or they will be forced to do so. However, that's for others to worry about. My focus right now is on the families of the dead and getting this lab up and running again. Next question,"

"Do you think the attack had anything to do with you being a minority? Do you think the attack was done by a white person?"

"That too would not surprise me, what with white privilege being what it is in this country," Morris wanted to hit on all the buzzwords so he could make everyone even angrier than they already were.

"What else was this particular building with all of its labs working on?" asked Hill.

"Our other labs were focused on explosives that are to be used on the moon for mining, but we have backup facilities for that. One of our labs worked on technology that if implanted in humans would get rid of the need of credit cards and paper money. Basically, we're working on technologies that make life easier." Morris glanced at the time on his tablet, and continued, "Okay, that's all the time I have to answer your questions. Thank you again for sending your drones. Good day." The drones flew away and the interview would be on the six o'clock news.

"Are we ready to begin?" asked Barker of Warren.

"You bet. Let's get Warren ready to attend a Sooners game."

Chapter 6

Warren woke up when Barker shook him awake. “Hey, wake up, we’re here,”

Warren opened his eyes, not entirely sure where “here” was. He could’ve sworn that he’d been kidnapped, but now he wasn’t so sure. “Uh, where are we?”

“Don’t you remember? We’re on Morris’ private jet, we just landed in Oklahoma City because you wanted to see a football game between the Sooners and the Buckeyes,” Barker wasn’t entirely sure this trick would work and hoped Warren didn’t see through it.

“I did?” Warren didn’t recall wanting to go see a football game, since he rarely wanted to spend his time surrounded by lots and lots of people. He didn’t care about being an alumni of Ohio State, even though he followed the football program, so to say he was confused would be an understatement.

“Yes, you did. Morris thought you seemed stressed out because of what happened to the lab. He wanted me to come with you because I’m the doctor of the group and he wanted me to make sure you came back relaxed,”

"Well, if you say so. I thought something else happened to me, like being kidnapped in the middle of the night. Maybe I was just too stressed out from the building being destroyed and it was probably just a nightmare I had. So, who did Morris blame for the building being destroyed?"

Ignoring the comment about being kidnapped, Barker replied, "He didn't really blame anyone, he implied that it was a combination of domestic terrorism, religious extremism, and white privilege. The media was happy to run with those ideas and make it sound way worse than it really was,"

"Oh, okay. What about the nanobots and the viruses, has that been implemented yet?"

"The bots will be activated in the next few hours. We should see the results shortly afterwards,"

"Great." Both men fell silent and remained that way until they reached the stadium.

At the stadium, they bought the tickets and went inside. The stadium wasn't as crowded like it normally would be because of all the chaos around the country due to racial strife and Oklahoma was just as affected by it. Barker was satisfied that there were more than enough victims to spread the nanobots everywhere and he was confident that the programming would prevent many of the bots from activating too soon. There was an added benefit of the game being on television, making Barker hope that seeing hundreds of people get sick would add to the psychological effect of the coming epidemic. Shortly before halftime, Barker would send an activation signal to the nanobots that were already inside Warren so the machines could get to work. After buying drinks and some snacks, the two found their seats in the opposing teams section of the stadium and waited for the game to begin.

Barker wasn't very interested in the game, so he browsed on his cell phone for a bit. At first, Warren didn't really seem all that interested either in the game, until Ohio State began racking up points and getting a big lead in the first quarter. When the game reached the two-minute mark in the second quarter, Barker decided it was time to activate the nanobots. Using an app on his cell phone, he sent the code to the microscopic machines and the display showed them waking up one by one. It took less than a minute for the nanobots to begin working, including replicating and going airborne.

Five minutes later, the game went to halftime, so Warren said, "Hey, I'm going to get a hotdog, do you want anything?"

"No, I'm good."

"Okay, I'll be right back."

Barker watched Warren walk away and thought, *Nope, you won't be back. The effects of the virus should start any minute now....*

Warren found a long line for the food counter, so he decided to wait. Without warning, he felt like he was hit in the head with a sledgehammer, followed by severe muscle pain throughout his body, enough to make him double over and collapse to the ground. Most people walked around him, trying not to pay attention to the writhing freak on the ground. One man decided to do something, bent down, and asked Warren, "Hey buddy, you okay?"

Before Warren could reply, he felt a tremendous pain in his stomach, and before the man who tried to assist him knew what was happening, Warren threw up all over him. Other football fans backed away, and the man replied, "Gross, now you've ruined my favorite jersey. I guess I'm going to have to call someone to bring me some fresh clothes, and I'll probably miss the rest of the game. Does anyone know if there's a medical room anywhere around here?" Then he glanced at the others fans gathered near him, mostly because of morbid fascination, so he said to them, "Come on, people, this guy needs some help. Does anyone want to help him out by going to find a nurse or whatever?"

Before anyone could respond, Warren screamed out in pain, followed by blood gushing from his eyes, mouth, and nose. The sight of all that blood shocked the people gathered – some ran, some wanted to throw up, and one or two rushed to find security or a medical professional. Warren writhed on the floor in agony, with no one helping him, wasn't able to talk because his tongue hurt just as badly as the rest of his body, and he could feel his life slipping away. Before passing out from the intense pain, Warren thought, *This is Barker and Morris' fault, they infected me with the bots and I have no way of warning people. Oh God, please let me die!*

Barker was watching from a corner, pleased with the real world results from the nanobots. When he saw Warren pass out, he walked over to the unconscious man, and said to those who were still lingering, "I think this man has the Ebola virus. We need to get him to the hospital immediately! Someone call 9-1-1,"

The reaction from the bystanders to hearing that Warren had Ebola was one of terror. Within fifteen minutes, the entire stadium heard about the virus and panic filled the air, with no sense of order left. Barker patiently waited for the stadium officials and the medical team to come see what was happening. Ten people approached Barker, they looked to him like a mixture of security, administration, and medical. One of them said to him, “Hello, I’m Doctor Mir Singh, head of the medical facility at this stadium. Are you a doctor?”

Deciding to lie, Barker replied, “Me? I’m only a lowly veterinarian. Luke Holt, at your service,”

“Oh, okay, Mr. Holt. Um, we’ve heard some disturbing news about this man’s condition. Is it true? Does he have Ebola?”

“Yes, I believe he does, or at least he did, because he died a few minutes ago. As to what happened, all I know is that he collapsed and displayed all the symptoms of Ebola. I know this because I was in the military during the Liberian outbreak and we had to help the local medical professionals deal with the disease. You’re going to need to do something about the people in this stadium before they spread it everywhere,”

“We should probably cancel the game,” replied one of the NCAA officials.

“I think that would be a wise decision. I’ll get on the intercom and try to get everyone to stay in the stadium. We need security to try to close the gates and lockdown this facility, although it might be too late, but we'll do the best we can." Singh turned to the President of the university, "Mr. Wagner, can you call the Norman Police and Fire Departments to cordon off the stadium?"

"I'll do that right away." Wagner rushed off towards the main office.

"All right, Mr. Holt, follow me, and we'll access the stadium's intercom system."

After the game was cancelled, Singh used the intercom and announced, "Attention everyone in this stadium. We are going to put this stadium under lockdown and put everyone in isolation. Please remain where you are. We cannot have this outbreak reach the general population. Please make your way to the field and my medical staff will do their best to keep you comfortable. We have alerted the authorities in Norman and they will stop you if you attempt to leave. When we have more information, we'll let you know. That is all."

The majority of the fans that were still in the stadium ignored Doctor Singh, rushed the gates, tore them down, completely ignored the warnings from stadium security, and headed for their cars. Only about ten percent of the people in the stadium actually stayed where they were. The police and fire departments couldn't stop everyone who managed to get away. The nanobots initiated the virus quickly and efficiently, causing some people to die within minutes of the bots entering their bodies. It wouldn't be too long before the city of Norman became a ghost town, followed by Oklahoma City, and then the main cities of the state.

Barker was pleased with the result so far, so he called Morris, "Mr. Morris, this is Joseph Barker. The bots worked like a charm. We already have about a dozen people dead, while some of the affected have left the stadium and are spreading the bots as we speak. The stadium personnel tried to lockdown the facility, but very few of the fans followed their directions. We had the added benefit of television coverage, because many millions of people were witness to this tragedy. If we continue to let the bots replicate, the country should start seeing more problems in the coming days,"

"Excellent news, Barker. You've done a great job so far. Are you able to leave the stadium so you can return here?"

"I think so. I'll call you as soon as I arrive at the airport back home. Once I'm back at the office, we should call for a press conference so I can inform everyone what the World Health Organization plans to do about this new threat,"

"Good idea. Do you think anyone from stadium personnel will recognize you when you appear on TV?"

"Not a chance. They'll be dead within the hour, so we should have no problems."

"Excellent. Okay, I'll write up what you should say and whatever happens after that, should be interesting. I should let you go, see you later." The phone call ended.

Two hours later, Barker was back at the office. Morris handed him a sheet of paper and said, "The press conference will be in thirty minutes. We'll have various American and United Nations reps standing behind you while you talk, that way it shows how utterly serious we are about this situation. Here's what I want you to say,"

Barker looked it over, lifted an eyebrow, smiled, and replied, "Boy, that's creative, and it should set a lot of people off. Hopefully, what we're doing should cause enough chaos in this country so that the government will collapse, and then we can bring it into the world community. I don't know about you, but I look forward to that day,"

"So do I, Doctor, so do I. I want you to read this over a few times so you won't sound stilted and then we'll go meet the press."

"Yes, sir."

This time, actual humans from the press had assembled in person when Barker came into the room and went straight to the podium. Behind him, stood various officials of the many government agencies that had a stake in what was to happen in the near future. Taking a deep breath, Barker began, "Ladies and gentlemen of the press, thank you for being here today. I'm Doctor Joseph Barker, head of the World Health Organization. As you may know by now, there's been an outbreak of Ebola that started in Oklahoma, at the game between the Sooners and Buckeyes, and now has spread beyond the borders of Oklahoma. We're doing what we can to help the poor people affected by this horrible virus and we ask Americans and anyone who has been in contact with Americans that were infected to do their best to stay away from Ebola victims. The World Health Organization, in conjunction with the CDC and American healthcare officials, will do our best to limit this outbreak and contain it before it affects the whole world.

"Now, what you may not know is that Christian terrorists from the American south were responsible for this attack. We have evidence that shows they were planning the attack for many months and used the black market to obtain the Ebola virus. The man they used as the suicide bomber, so to speak, was a well-known anti-government type who was inciting the people in his group to overthrow the rightful government of the United States. They also want to dismantle the United Nations because they feel the UN is a threat to the world. These are also the same people responsible for the attacks on foreign owned businesses across the country and we feel that these people are a threat to the mental and physical health of the nation, and maybe even the world. The United States government officials standing behind me will detail what'll happen next as far as these terrorists are concerned. We'll take questions once we're done speaking. Next to speak, is Deputy FBI director Yusef Aberdin."

The obviously Muslim man came to the podium and began, "Thank you, Doctor Barker. As the doctor just said, white Christian terrorists, especially of the southern variety, are responsible for the spread of Ebola here in this country. I'm here to ask my fellow citizens to begin reporting on the activity of all Christians across this country to their local FBI and DHS offices and to immediately report anything you might find suspicious. For too long, they've gotten away with rejecting government authority over marriage, what they can and can't say in the podium at their churches, educating their children at home, and for rejecting the government's authority over their very lives. They even have the audacity to continue to celebrate and honor the so-called Rebel Flag and the long dead, so-called heroes from their past, when all of us know that doing such a thing is racist.

"With the help of good American citizens, like those of you watching, we can make our country great again by gathering up these religious bio-terrorists and punishing them for their wrongheaded ideas and attempts to destroy their fellow man. To contact us when you see a problem, you can visit our website to send an email, call the phone number listed the site, or you can visit us in person to report any suspicious activity. All right, now we'll take questions."

The questions from the press were pre-determined and so were the answers. What most people took away from the press conference was that American Christians were responsible for all the ills of the United States and that they must be held responsible for every single problem the country currently was going through.

Unbeknownst to Barker, Morris, and the rest, they had no idea Satan and his forces were manipulating them, and were chomping at the bit to take full control of the Earth whenever God allowed it. As it was, the darkness of sin and evil was slowly enveloping the entire planet. Christians with discernment could see what was happening and they prayed for the rapture to happen soon.

Chapter 7

Meanwhile, Tim Richman continued to burn down foreign owned businesses. At home, his wife had absolutely no idea what he was up to and Tim thought no one else knew either. It bothered him that now some of those foreigners were paying back Americans by burning down American owned businesses in retaliation, but Tim thought that sometimes painful things had to be done to change the direction of the country back towards what he nostalgically thought it was when he was a child.

Tim and Donna watched the news conference highlights on the ten o'clock local news about the sudden spread of the Ebola virus and who the officials blamed it on, to which Donna said, "They're blaming Christians for the virus and the destruction of foreign owned businesses? That's the dumbest thing I've ever heard. I'd believe Muslims doing that sort of thing over some random Christian doing that,"

"That's probably because those Christians make themselves easy targets, mostly because they don't fight back, and would rather preach. Anyway, did it seem like that FBI guy implied that Southerners in general were the problem?"

"I guess so. Is it because we prefer the government and its control freaks to stay out of our lives so we can live the way we want without interference?"

"I'd say so. It wasn't too long ago that some of those so-called social justice warriors went after the Rebel flag along with anything associated with the Confederacy, and managed to get their way to some extent. Now I imagine there'll be a full-on assault against Southern culture and probably Christians after this Ebola scare. Since you're a nurse, have you seen any indications of Ebola at your work?"

"Not yet, but we're doing our best to prepare. Although, I'm not sure how effective our preparations will be if this new strain is as deadly as they say it is, but it is what it is. How's your work search coming along?"

"About as well as could be expected, but most of these employers seem to prefer the cheap labor that Uncle Sam is encouraging them to hire, but I'm sure someone will hire me pretty soon. Maybe I ought to try applying for a job at Sol System Mining,"

"Sol System Mining?" Donna had a confused look on her face.

"Have you forgotten about that new mining venture on the moon already? The next story on the news is an update about it,"

"Oh, right. Why would you want to work for them?"

"I don't, but it would be cool to see Earth from the moon and go into space,"

"And leave me here all by myself?"

"I wouldn't do that, I'd only go if I could take you with me, since you are the love of my life after all,"

"Aw, that's sweet of you to say. I love you too," she kissed him.

"Hey, that update's coming up, let's watch,"

The news anchor began, "As you know, Sol System Mining sent up mining equipment, supplies, and a whole team of engineers and miners to the moon to begin drilling for water for the new colony on the surface and for minerals we could use here back on Earth. The head of the team, Simon Anderson, has updated their progress and we have the video he posted on their website earlier in the day,"

The video began playing and showed Anderson in a spacesuit, but without a helmet, and looked like he was sitting in the cockpit of the moon lander. He began, "Greetings everyone and thanks for watching our weekly update. As you know, we had a successful launch and landing two weeks ago and we're nearly finished with setting up the mining equipment to extract the water and minerals from the dark side of the moon. We expect great success as every probe that's tested for water has returned results that look incredibly promising and will help maintain future colonies on the moon. The probes have also indicated the moon is rich in mineral deposits, so we hope to extract what we can and send the material back to Earth. If this proves successful, the company will begin looking into doing the same on Mars. That's it for this week, stay tuned for more updates as we continue this historic mission. This is Simon Anderson on the dark side of the moon, signing off."

The news continued with an item about Pope Peter asking for a meeting between him and the leaders of all the world's religions at the United Nations building in New York. Tim ignored it, and said, "That's cool about being able to mine on the moon. I wonder when we'll finally have ships that'll leave the solar system?"

"Your guess is as good as mine, Dear." Donna yawned. "You know, I have an early day tomorrow since it's Monday, so I'm going to bed. Goodnight, Tim."

"Goodnight, Sweetheart." They kissed and she went to bed.

Tim waited for an hour before he decided to continue his mission. Once he verified his wife was fast asleep, he went to the garage to gather all the items he needed, and then put them in his truck's bed. As he drove away from the house, he hoped his next target was still standing, since so many people had joined his cause to burn down businesses of foreigners.

After traveling for an hour on the confusing chaos that was the highway system in the Dallas-Fort Worth Metroplex, Tim finally came to his target, a foreign owned grocery store near Alliance Airport. Because he'd been doing this for a while and hadn't been caught, Tim was getting sloppy, so much so that he parked his truck in the grocery store's parking lot when he normally parked it a few blocks away. The parking lot itself was ringed with active security cameras positioned on the lights lighting up the lot, some of which picked up his activity. He was also overconfident, so he had stopped paying as much attention to his surroundings. Tim got out of his truck, opened the tailgate to take out the fuel for the fire, along with some other equipment, and headed for the stores' entrance.

Tim opened the gas can and was about to pour when he heard guns being cocked. From the darkness, someone ordered, "Stop right there, put the gas can down, and put your hands up,"

Turning around, Tim saw three men in security guard outfits with shotguns pointed at him. He put the can down and raised his hands. "I guess you caught me. I would've never figured a closed grocery store would have security guards. I guess there's a first time for everything,"

The man that had ordered Tim to put down the gas can, said, "Normally, they wouldn't, but the owners of this place have other properties that were destroyed, so they hired our security operation to protect their other assets. Okay, now the cops are on their way. If you try anything, we won't hesitate to shoot you full of lead. Put your hands behind your back so we can tie them together."

Tim's answer was a shrug, he did what they told him to do, and then had him sit on the ground. Tim thought to himself while they tied his hands and frisked him, *I'm surprised I got away with this for as long as I did. I wonder what Donna's gonna do when she finds out? I guess I'll find out in a few hours.*

The cops arrived with not only their squad cars, but with a SWAT armored vehicle tagging along, and with news vans of the local media following not far behind.

The drones the media used would've been useless in the darkness. Once the police cars parked, Tim ended up surrounded by officers who didn't look all that happy because they were being followed by the bright lights of television cameras. The senior ranking officer walked up to the guard who stopped Tim, and said, "Good job, Ryan. Your firms' patience finally paid off. Tell me who we have here,"

"Well, according to the license I pulled from his wallet, this is forty-year-old Tim Richman of Plano,"

The police officer bent down to speak to Tim, "So, Mr. Richman, you're under arrest. Since you're obviously an American citizen, we'll assume you already know your Miranda Rights, so I won't bother with them, unless you feel it's absolutely necessary that I do so. Get to your feet and we'll take you to jail."

Before they could get too far, the bright lights from the news cameras practically blinded Tim because it was the middle of the night and he'd gotten used to the darkness. With his hands behind his back, he had no way to shield his eyes, but because of the shadows that were cast from the darkness and the lights, the cameras had a hard time getting a clear picture of Tim's face. Even though he couldn't see anyone, he heard questions being shouted at him about why he did it, but the police told the assembled media their questions would be answered later. The officer roughly put Tim in the back seat of his vehicle and a few minutes later, they were off to the police station.

At the station, they fingerprinted Tim, took his mugshot, and led him to a somewhat full jail cell. Before the officer walked away, Tim asked, "Don't I get a phone call? You know, so I can call my lawyer or whatever?"

"You do realize it's the middle of the night, everybody's probably asleep, so there ain't anybody who's gonna answer the phone. You can wait 'til morning." The officer walked out of sight.

Tim felt like a caged animal and started pacing, which annoyed the others in the cell with him, but he settled down after about an hour. He sat down next to a man who seemed at peace. The man smiled and said, "Hi, I'm Pastor Sam Rogers. So, what are you accused of doing?"

"Hey, I'm Tim Richman. You're a pastor? That's sort of interesting. You asked what I'm accused of? I don't think they've accused me of it yet, but they finally caught me attempting to burn down a foreign owned business,"

Rogers raised his eyebrows, and asked, “Were you the one who started burning down those businesses?”

“Yup, that’s me, but I wasn’t expecting such a huge backlash from it. I guess that’s what I get for not thinking things through,”

“The Bible says that your sins will find you out, sometimes sooner than other times,”

“If that’s true, then what kind of sin did you do to get thrown in here?”

“I’m here because the powers-that-be wanted to make an example of Christians. If you’d like, I can tell you what happened yesterday and how I ended up here.”

“All right, not like I have anywhere to go at the moment."

Chapter 8

Earlier the previous day…..

Pastor Rogers wasn't sure how many of his congregation would show up for Sunday services at his house. The latest news claiming Christians were to blame for Ebola had everyone in his congregation jumpy and somewhat paranoid that the government would come after them. Rogers had to admit to himself that the government arresting him was a distinct possibility, but he thought it would be much further down the road. Whatever happened, he knew God was in control, so Rogers wasn't too worried about his personal safety. When the Sunday morning service started at 10:45, nearly every member of his church were in their places, ready to hear him preach, with the exception of Doctor Kirkland. Kirkland was at work at the hospital, where one weekend a month he had to work on Saturday and Sunday, otherwise, he'd show up every time there was a service. Rogers was happy that this latest convert to Christ was taking his relationship with Christ seriously.

Everything changed fifteen minutes into the service.

Since the church service took place in Rogers' personal home, he heard many vehicles coming onto his property and it sounded like a whole lot of people had arrived. Without interrupting the congregations' singing, Rogers got up and looked out the front window. What he saw disturbed him. There were a dozen police SWAT outside who seemed to be backed up by dozens of obvious gay people and what looked like a couple of Muslims behind them. Rogers thought, *What a motley crew Satan has. Lord, please help me to stand up to the forces of evil and if it's in your will that my congregation and I die today, let it be quick so we can be with you in Heaven in an instant.*

Before Rogers even thought to open the door, he heard an order come through loudspeaker, "Attention inside. Come out with your hands up. You have five minutes to comply before we storm in. Five minutes begins now,"

Rogers heard the congregation stop singing. Erika came to him and asked, "What's going on?"

"I'm not sure, but I think the government is finally coming after Christians to get us out of the way,"

"What do you want to do? Should I go get your guns?"

"No, we're outgunned and outnumbered. If we attempt to fight back, that'll only make the situation worse. Get the congregation together to pray while I go outside to speak with whoever's in charge,"

"Be careful. I love you."

"I'll do my best. I love you too." The two hugged and kissed briefly. After his wife left his side, Pastor Rogers took a deep breath and went outside.

Stepping outside, Rogers raised his arms above his head, partially because that's what he was ordered to do and partially because of the multiple automatic rifles pointed his way. Rogers spoke, trying not to sound afraid, "All right, I'm Sam Rogers, the pastor here, but this is also private property and I'd like to know what this is about before I ask you to leave,"

The man in charge of the SWAT team was about to say something, but was interrupted by a woman who was dressed like a man, whose hair was cut like a man's, and whose body language implied that she was one, but her voice still sounded like a woman's. She walked up to Rogers with hate in her eyes, an angry scowl on her face, and said, "We're here to finally do something about you so-called Christians. You know, we've tried suing your businesses, getting the Supreme Court to make you marry us in your churches, we've tried jailing you to make you do what the law of the land says, and we have even tried shutting down your places of worship, but you keep persisting in doing what you want and worshipping wherever you please. Now, your kind is infecting all of us with the Ebola virus, and maybe you're even burning down foreign owned businesses, so now we've come to finally put an end to this impasse we've found ourselves. Where's the rest of your people?"

"Why does it bother you so much that we want to be free to associate with who we want, instead of being forced to associate with people we have nothing in common with? And why is it that you want us to tolerate your lifestyle, but you won't tolerate our beliefs?"

Ignoring his question, the woman asked, "Why aren't the others in your house coming out? We know they're in there,"

"Why do you hate us so much? I see that you're being backed my Muslims. You do know they kill gays, right? All we Christians do is tell you that God loves you and Jesus died for your sins, while they cut of your heads, throw you off buildings, and probably commit a host of other crimes against gays, so why not go after them?"

Continuing to ignore what Rogers was saying, the woman turned to the SWAT team, "Why don't you go in there and get all the people who haven't come out here yet?"

"All right. Men, storm the building, bring anyone inside out here."

A dozen armed men in black armor stormed Rogers' house. He heard shouting, but there was no gunfire. Less than five minutes later, all sixty members of his congregation were outside, including the Carson family. Many of the woman and children were teary-eyed, while a couple of the men in his congregation were defiant and looked like they wanted to take on the SWAT team in hand-to-hand combat. "Okay, we're all here. Now what are you going to do, take us to FEMA camps?"

The woman rolled her eyes at the mention of the FEMA camps, saying, "Oh, brother, that conspiracy theory again. Why on earth would we waste money and resources on you people?" Then she turned around and spoke to the Muslims, "You're free to do want you want now, but keep Pastor Rogers alive, we need him for further questioning. The rest of us will set fire to the house."

A dozen Muslim men approached the Christians with long swords in their hands and a gleeful sort of smile on their faces.

Rogers heard his people praying for strength so they wouldn't be afraid to face their impending deaths and he silently prayed for the strength to endure whatever was going to happen to him and that he'd be a strong witness for Christ in the coming days. He looked over at his wife, who had tears in her eyes. Erika smiled back at him and mouthed that she loved him. Rogers replied the same way and he was thankful that he was married to such a strong Christian.

Two SWAT members approached Rogers and cuffed his hands behind his back. The adults were doing their best to remain stoic, but the dozen children, all under ten, were crying. The scene broke Rogers' heart. They made him watch as the Muslims used long, sharp knives to cut off the heads of his congregation, including Erika's. The gay men and women who had come with the SWAT and Muslims cheered when the heads of the Christians were removed from their bodies, while they poured gasoline around the perimeter of the house so they could set fire to it. Although his eyes filled with tears seeing the headless bodies and he quietly mourned for them, Rogers knew he'd see his friends and wife again in Heaven. He looked forward to it, even though he would've liked the Rapture to occur at that very moment so he could skip everything that was about to happen to him.

Before they put him into the back of the SWAT van, he said, “You may think you’ve won, but God will win in the end. I’ll pray for your souls so that all of you will see the error of your ways before it’s too late….”

“Shut up.” interrupted one of the SWAT team members as he punched Rogers in the gut with the butt of his rifle, forcibly made Rogers to sit on the bench in the van, and roughly handcuffed his hands to the wall to prevent him from being able to move.

The last thing Rogers saw from the van was his house, the home he’d built for his family many years ago, go up in flames. Although sad that his family’s memories were disappearing, he was glad that once he was in heaven, such trivial earthly matters would no longer bother him. Once he was at the jail, they made him change into orange prison garb and put him into a jail cell full of other prisoners.

“So, that’s how I came to be in this jail. I suspect my kangaroo trial will happen any day now,” Rogers said to Tim Richman.

“And that doesn’t worry you?”

“Not at all. With Christ as my Lord and Savior, I know where I’ll be when I die. It really doesn’t matter what happens to my body, since my soul will be with the Lord in Heaven when I die,"

"So, I guess you knowing Jesus is why you seem so calm and not panicky?"

"Yes. I know in my heart He died for my sins and that I'll be with Him when I die. Now, according to John 3:16 in the Bible, God gave His only begotten son so that whosoever believed in Him should not perish but have everlasting life. In other words, I believed that He would forgive me of my sins, which He did, and now I know where I'll go when I die,"

"How can I get what you have? Is it hard? Do I have to go through some ritual?" Richman was concerned that he would have to go through some elaborate ceremony and if he had to do that, he wasn't sure he'd go through with it.

"Asking Jesus to save you from your sins isn't hard at all, it's really quite simple, and there's no ritual. All you have to do is confess to God that you're a sinner through prayer, then you follow that by asking Christ to forgive you of your sins, and then ask Him to save you from those sins so that you'll go to Heaven when you die. We call it being spiritually born again. Okay?"

"What if I make a mistake and sin more, do I need to pray that God will save me again or work harder so He'd let me go to Heaven?"

"We're human, we always sin, but once you show you're sincere about wanting to be saved from your sins, you'll always have that protection. You only have to ask for forgiveness when you've done wrong and no amount of works will be enough to save you. If it worked the way you and many others think, Jesus would have to constantly come to Earth to die for our sins, so His dying once worked forever. Do you understand?"

"I do. What-if I wanted to wait though, if say I wanted to clean up my life some more?"

"I wouldn't wait if I were you. You never know the day and hour of your death, and since you're in jail, that could come any day, even any minute, from now. You're probably as ready as you'll ever be at this moment in time,"

"All right, I'll go ahead and ask forgiveness for my sins, but what do I need to say?"

"Here's a prayer that I suggest people say, you can repeat it if you like or you could pray something simpler: Dear God in Heaven, I come to you in the name of Jesus. I acknowledge to you that I am a sinner, and I am sorry for my sins. I need your forgiveness. I believe that your only begotten Son, Jesus Christ, shed His precious blood on the cross at Calvary and died for my sins. With all of my heart, I believe that God raised Jesus from the dead. At this very moment, I accept Jesus Christ as my own personal Lord and Savior. Thank you, Jesus, for dying for me and giving me eternal life. Amen."

Richman repeated the prayer and felt God's presence for the first time ever in his life and he was grateful that he met Pastor Rogers. "Thank you for leading me to the Lord, Pastor, I really appreciate it,"

"You're welcome, I was glad to do it. I just wish I had a Bible to give you so you could study a little before your trial, but the Lord will give you strength in spite of that,"

I hope so,"

"Oh, He will." Rogers then noticed two of the other prisoners listening in on the conversation, he asked them, "Would you like to have Jesus come into your lives?"

One of the men walked away, not wanting to get further involved, while the other said, "You have your way to get to Heaven and I have my way,"

"It's not *my* way, you know, it's God's way, and there's no possible way you could do enough to save yourself so you can get to Heaven,"

"Whatever, man. You believe what you believe and I'll believe what I believe." He walked away.

Before Rogers could stop him, two guards came to the door of the cell, and one of them said, "We need Sam Rogers front and center,"

Sighing, Rogers replied from where he still sat, "I suppose I'm going to meet the judge already for my kangaroo trial?"

"Yes, so hurry it up, we don't have all day."

"Good luck, Pastor, I'll pray for you."

"Thanks, Tim. Well, off I go." Rogers stepped forward, the guards handcuffed him when they opened the cell door, and led him away.

Chapter 9

The guards led Rogers to the courthouse, which was across the street from the jail. Multiple media outlets had gathered outside the courthouse, including some drones hovering over the area. He assumed the media had assembled in force to report on his trial, not really thinking there were others on trial that the media thought were far more important than him. Many of their cameras focused on him and he heard various reporters shouting questions at him, some of which seemed to be completely random.

"Are you responsible for the Ebola virus?"

"Do you know where the rest of your terrorist faction is located?"

"Were you the one who burned down all those foreign owned businesses?"

Rogers realized he wasn't the entire focus of the media and thought to himself, *Maybe they think I'm Tim Richman or they really are here to report on what happens in my trial. Lord, please help me say the right things and show the people that Christians don't wilt in the face of persecution. Please give me the strength and wisdom to do what you need me to do. In your name, amen.*

When they led him into the courtroom, Rogers saw the gallery packed with spectators, along with representatives from the media. Again, he wondered if this was all for him or for everyone on trial that day. The guards led him to a table where he would obviously be sitting by himself, since whoever was in charge hadn't seen fit to provide him with counsel. There was also no jury in the jury box, which confirmed to him that it was definitely a kangaroo trial. When the judge finally came in, Rogers figured out who had jurisdiction here, and that was the federal government. That was because the judge was a federal district judge who'd been appointed years ago by a President of the United States who made no bones about being Communist, instead of being a member of either official party. This judge was renowned to be very hard on Christians, Conservatives, and anyone who preferred limited government.

Judge Samantha Boyd was nearing retirement age and wanted to have a bold, history-changing legacy that schoolchildren would learn about in their school history books decades and even centuries from now. When the President of the United States appointed her to this judgeship twenty years earlier, she set out to prove that Christians and anyone associated with them were troublemakers and needed to be stopped before doing more harm. Constitutional rights didn't matter to her and she never gave a moment's thought when it came to thinking she was being manipulated by unseen supernatural forces who wished to destroy the United States and its Christian heritage. Judge Boyd knew she enjoyed persecuting her and the states' enemies and that's all that mattered to her.

Rogers looked over at the table where the persecutor was standing. Instead of the city, county, or state of Texas prosecuting him, the Deputy Attorney General of the United States would do the honors. Rogers thought, *I don't know if I should be honored or terrified. These two show that the deck is stacked against the Christians on trial today and I'm pretty sure I already know my fate. Lord, I'm prepared to meet you in Heaven this very day if you require it of me.*

The Deputy Attorney General, Nathan McDowell, was a well-known donor to the Communist Party of the United States, which was the party currently in control of the White House and Congress, and he was once Mayor of Seattle. While Mayor of Seattle, McDowell had sued the traditional Christian churches, which were mostly small and lacked the money to fight back, for such things as not allowing gays to marry in their churches and for preaching against the federal government for being corrupt and led by sinners. Under McDowell's leadership, Seattle had removed all Christians from the city, destroyed their churches, and eventually the state of Washington followed suit. Because of McDowell's success, many communist leaning cities did the same to their Christian communities. Now, most of the Christians that survived were in the southern portion of the United States.

"All right, everyone be seated. Okay, I see that the case I have before me involves a Christian, a pastor to be specific. What are the charges, Mr. McDowell?"

"Your Honor, it's the same litany of charges every Christian I have ever prosecuted is accused of, which is refusing to follow the laws of the land. These accusations include everything from not paying their taxes on their church buildings, to not marrying gays in their churches, to criticizing the lawful government of the United States of America. There's only one outcome to this trial - the defendant is guilty and needs to be punished for his crimes,"

"The outcome is still to be determined, Mr. McDowell. Now, Mr. Samuel J. Rogers, please approach the stand." Rogers took the stand and the judge continued, "You've heard the charges against you, what defense do you provide?"

"First of all, don't I get access to a lawyer, or even a public defender? I mean, I would think you'd want this trial to look legit, instead of obviously looking like a kangaroo trial," Rogers heard some of the audience behind him laugh.

Judge Boyd reached for her gavel and used it to bring order to the courtroom. Then she looked like she took a deep breath, and said, "A public defender is not necessary, because I believe you can defend yourself. Many of your kind claim your God gives you the strength and the ability to speak beyond your supposed limitations, so we would like to see that put into action. Now, defend yourself,"

Rogers shrugged and replied, "All right, I'm guilty. You have your verdict, now you can get rid of me,"

"You're not going to get off that easily, Mr. Rogers. You will answer each accusation the United States government has brought before this court. Are we clear?"

"Yes, Your Honor,"

"First, the Supreme Court declared many years ago that gays had the right marry and had the right to be married by whomever they asked. They also have the right to be served by anyone they ask and cannot be refused that service, for example having a wedding cake be made for their special occasion. While I may know your answer to this question, I'd like for those here in the courtroom and those at home watching on their television or mobile devices to hear what you have to say. So, please give your reasons for not doing what the government asks all of its citizens to do,"

"Well, I believe the United States government is not the ultimate authority. I believe that my God is the authority in all things in this life and I have to answer to Him when I die,"

"What-if we said we didn't believe in your God?" asked McDowell.

"You may not, but He does believe in you, so much so that He gave His only begotten son to die for your sins. The Bible says that all have sinned and have come short of the glory of God. It also says the wages of sin is death, but the gift of God is eternal life,"

"What nonsense. Why do you hate gays so much?"

"Why do you hate Christians?"

"Answer the question, Mr. Rogers," ordered Boyd. "And please remember that you're not here to ask Mr. McDowell questions,"

"I don't hate gays. I hate the sin they commit because they're going against God's natural laws for men and women, but I don't personally hate anyone,"

"The government says gays can marry, so why don't you marry them?"

"For one thing, they've never come to me and asked, mostly because I stopped marrying people who were not members of my church, but I would've said no anyway if gays had asked me. For another, God says that only male and female can marry because they produce offspring. The last time I looked, gays don't do that, at least not without lots of help. If we continue to allow such unnatural acts to occur, God's judgment will fall on this country, if it hasn't already, and I wouldn't want to be here when that happens,"

"What a pathetic excuse for not wanting members of our community to be happy. Why do you continue to defy the United States government?"

"What do you mean?"

"Why don't you pay the property tax for your church buildings?"

"We meet in my home, so I do pay property taxes. Maybe if you had done a little research on my background, you would know that,"

"Mr. Rogers, no need to be sarcastic," admonished Judge Boyd.

"Sorry,"

"What about before you met in your home, I'm sure you used to have a church building and property. Correct?" asked McDowell.

"Of course, but that's before the church in general lost tax exempt status. When that happened, we sold the building and property and moved to my house for services,"

"I see. All right, what about terrorism?"

"Terrorism? I don't understand,"

"Do you know anyone responsible for the terrorism that caused the Ebola virus to spread like wildfire across the globe?"

"No and that's not something a Christian would do. What about the Muslims? They've been spreading their particular brand of hate for centuries, including destroying priceless historical pieces and killing millions, why don't you put one of them on trial?"

"What you're referring to are a small band of misguided people who claim to be Muslims, but the vast majority is peace-loving and would do nothing to harm their fellow mankind,"

"You only say that because some of your masters are Muslim and they'd behead you for saying anything contrary to that,"

"Mr. Rogers, you're coming close to contempt of court and you're becoming combative, please mind yourself," ordered Boyd.

Rogers really wanted to say something sarcastic back to the judge, but it would not help his cause as a Christian for those watching at home, even though the outcome to this trial was clear. Taking a deep breath so he could try to remain calm, he replied, "Yes, ma'am,"

McDowell continued the questioning, "Why is it so important to you to follow Jesus that you'll risk going to jail?"

"I believe Jesus died for my sins when He came to Earth two thousand years ago. Because of His sacrifice, I'll go to Heaven when I die. God set out what He wants from us in the Bible and I believe that if you don't do what He wants and if you don't follow Him, you'll go to Hell when you die,"

"So if I or anyone else doesn't believe in this God or Jesus, we would be sent to this Hell?"

"Yes, because you rejected Him, whether you did it knowingly or unknowingly,"

"So, we'll go to Hell because of our supposed unbelief?"

"Unfortunately, yes you will,"

“What about anyone who has not heard of this Jesus? Would you punish them?”

“I’m not punishing them. They will go to Hell, but that’s more the believer’s fault than the sinner who hadn’t heard. We’re tasked with going into the world and preaching to every person, so that’s a major failure on the Christian’s part for letting anyone die without knowing Jesus as their Savior. Jesus came not to condemn the world, but to save it,”

“Uh huh. So you don’t think there are many ways to this Heaven of yours?”

“No, sir, just the one,”

“Then you disagree with Pope Peter. He’s declared there are many ways to Heaven and has said that your sect is wrong,”

“He’s welcome to think whatever he wants, but he does not speak for God, even if he claims he does,”

“So you don’t think everyone that does some good in their lives, like giving back to their community, goes to Heaven?”

“No,”

“Why not?”

“If everyone got to go to Heaven because they gave to charity or built homes for the homeless, then it wouldn’t be special, because they’re still sinners in God’s eyes. Would you want to go to a special place that's supposed to be reserved to a select few if everyone was able to go too and they were pretty much exactly the same way as they were on Earth? Sort of like an exclusive country club that you're probably a member of, Mr. McDowell. You wouldn't want a guy like me there, would you?"

Ignoring the question, McDowell asked, "So, you're willing to go against the head of your church and millions of others who follow the Pope?"

"He's not the head of my church, Jesus is. The Pope and others like him are the leaders of millions who would follow these so-called leaders off a cliff if any of them says that's what God wants. Men like the Pope lead churches who would rather be popular with the world, and because of that, I'd consider them apostates. The followers of the these powerful men are like the sheep who would be led to slaughter and wouldn't know it until it was too late. As far as I can tell, this Pope could very well be the false prophet to the anti-Christ,"

"False prophet? Anti-Christ? Please elaborate, Mr. Rogers,"

"Well, during a seven year period called Tribulation, the false prophet will convince people, through a mass delusion, that an enigmatic leader in world politics is Christ. The false prophet will convince people to worship this leader. While in power, this anti-Christ will usher in many wars and will reign over a planet that will go through seven trumpet and seven bowl judgments that's supposed to cleanse the planet of those who do not believe in the real Jesus Christ. If you heard the Christian message before this period, you will not be able to repent, but there will be many who haven't heard who will repent of their sins. To those of you watching, I might be your only chance to hear about Jesus and His dying for your sins on the cross….."

"I think that's enough." interrupted McDowell. "Your Honor, I think we've gone about as far as we can with Mr. Rogers. He obviously won't recognize the authority of the State, or recant his beliefs, and he seems to think Jesus is the end all of everything. I suggest we proceed to the judgment phase of this trial,"

"I think you're right, Mr. McDowell. Mr. Rogers, you have been found guilty and your punishment is death by beheading. The execution will take place tomorrow morning, alongside other condemned prisoners. So ends the trial of Samuel Rogers. Guards escort him back to the jail. We will have the next trial in an hour." Boyd banged the gavel, ending the trial, and she went back to her chambers. The guards escorted Rogers to a cellblock in the jail for convicted felons that were set for the death penalty. Rogers decided to spend the next few hours of his life in prayer.

Chapter 10

Donna Richman watched the trial on television, fascinated by the reasons some of the criminals gave for doing whatever it was the government accused them of doing. Even though she gave the trials most of her attention, she was worried about her husband, not knowing where he'd gone off to, since she hadn't seen him since the night before. Because he seemed to have disappeared, Donna got off work early. She hoped he wasn't cheating on her or had somehow gotten mixed up with the wrong crowd and was now lying in some ditch somewhere, bleeding to death.

The doorbell rang just as Rogers' trial ended, so Donna got up from the couch to answer the door, grateful that she didn't have the opportunity to think about that Christian and his being unfairly treated by the powers-that-be. Opening her door, the last thing she expected was two police officers, nor was she expecting to see drones flying above her house, and the dozen or so reporters on her lawn.

"Ma'am, I'm Officer Ethan Reid of the Plano Police Department. Are you Tim Richman's wife Donna?"

"Uh, yes, sir. What's this about?"

"Well, your husband is in jail, accused of being a domestic terrorist,"

"What?" Donna couldn't believe what she was hearing.

"We have your husband in custody because we believe he's the one who started the terrorism against particular businesses in the area. His trial is set to begin in a few hours and since we know he didn't use his one phone call, we thought we should come out here and inform you of the situation ourselves,"

Shocked, Donna wasn't sure what to do now. "Should I go visit him before his trial?"

"That's up to you, ma'am. We can escort you there so the media won't bother you, if you'd like,"

"Uh, okay. Wouldn't escorting me be too much trouble? I mean, don't you have better things to do?"

"Escorting you wouldn't be any trouble at all, because it's part of what we do. Do you need to do anything before we go?"

"No, sir. I'll turn off the TV and then I'll get my purse. Do I follow you in my car?"

"Yes, ma'am. We'll get the press to back off so you can leave your driveway and then we'll go to the jail."

"Okay."

The officers managed to get the assembled press to back off, but couldn't get the people who controlled the drones to get the machines to leave the area. Donna nervously started her car, backed out of the garage, and into the street. Two police cars were waiting for her – one was to stay in front of her and the other followed. The media followed, doing their best to get the story or make it up on the fly to keep their ratings high as they continually broadcast live on-air.

At the jail, the police escorted Donna to the jail cell where her husband was. By this time, there were fewer people in jail, so she could easily find Tim, who was still sitting on a bench. The guard said, "Mr. Richman, your wife is here to see you."

Tim looked up and saw that his wife was standing in front of the cell. He wasn't happy about his situation and wasn't entirely sure how Donna would react. He got up and approached where she stood, saw that she had been crying, and said, "Hey, Donna,"

"Tim, they're accusing you of being a domestic terrorist and they wouldn't tell me exactly what you'd done. What did you do?"

"I over-reacted to losing my job, so I burned down a few businesses owned by foreigners. I so very much regret doing that now,"

"I hope you do. What are we going to do now? You should've known they would've found you and they'll probably find you guilty. I hope they won't execute you tomorrow morning,"

"I know they will, but I'm pretty sure they will execute me. You see, I converted to Christianity,"

"What?" Donna was dumbfounded; she thought her husband was more rational than that.

"I was led to Jesus by a pastor that was in here a few hours ago shortly before they took him to court. What he said made a lot of sense to me,"

Tim could see Donna's mood change, from feeling hurt to anger. "Why on earth would you let a nut job like that convince you to follow all of that nonsense? Are you so afraid to face the consequences of your actions that you'd fall for anything just to get you out of it?"

"That's not it at all. I now believe Jesus died for my sins so I could go to Heaven when I die. I'm more than willing to face the consequences to my previous actions in court because what I did was wrong and I admit it. Can't you be happy for me that I accepted Jesus into my heart and I'm going to face up to my wrongdoing?"

"No, because what you did before and what you did now makes no sense to me at all. If we had time, I'd take you to a psychologist to find out what's wrong with you, but we can't. You know, I don't think I know who you are anymore, so this will definitely be the last time you see me. Goodbye." Donna turned and walked away.

Tim felt stunned and baffled by his wife's reaction. He wanted to go after her, but being stuck behind bars limited what he could do. "Wait! Please don't go!" He shouted, trying to get her attention. It didn't do any good, she left the room. Tim went back to the bench with tears in his eyes so he could pray that someone who believed in Jesus would seek his wife out and lead her to the Lord before it was too late.

Hours went by before the guards escorted Tim to the courthouse. Like the others before him that had gone to trial, the media outside of the building attempted to ask him questions, mostly asking why he burned down all those buildings. He was sure that they would know all about him by the end of the trial and would broadcast to the world everything they knew about him – from his marriage to losing his job to his late conversion to Christ. If Tim gauged the mood right, the public would demand his execution just for being a Christian, since he was considered a domestic terrorist, so being a Christian on top of that would be icing on the cake for them.

Once in the courtroom, Tim found that it packed with spectators, including the media. His guards led him to a table and made him stand as everyone waited for Judge Boyd. Boyd's reputation preceded her, because even Tim knew who she was when she entered the courtroom, so he knew this trial would be quick because Boyd was not one to put up with nonsense in her courtroom. Since the time of day was near normal end of day business hours, he could tell Boyd was tired, so she was probably lacking patience and would be irritable. The bailiff told everyone to sit and the trial began.

"Prosecutor McDowell, let's make this last case quick. Who do we have before us now?"

"Your Honor, this is Tim Richman. He has a couple of accusations against him. First, he's accused of being the first to burn down the businesses of some of our newest Americans,"

"I see. Mr. Richman, why'd you do it?"

"I guess I did it because I was angry that I lost my job to an illegal,"

"So you lost your job to an undocumented immigrant, it's not a big deal. That happens every day to various people, yet they don't destroy other peoples' livelihoods. Because of you, we have multiple businesses owned by English and non-English speaking citizens being destroyed in retribution and the authorities are having a hard time putting a stop to it,"

"I'm sorry, I didn't think it would go as far as it did,"

"I'd say that was pretty accurate – you didn't think. I'd also say it was too late for apologies now. You should have thought before you acted. You can guarantee your white male privilege won't get you off, so don't look forward to that,"

What white privilege? I've never gotten anything because I'm white. I've had to work hard for everything I've ever gotten. What a ridiculous thing to say. Tim thought to himself. He was angry with himself for doing what he did and he was angry that he was in front of a very biased judge who was not particularly fond of whites or the male gender, if she still believed in fixed genders. Tim decided to keep his mouth shut, instead of responding to her obvious hate.

"All right, Mr. McDowell, what was the other charge you said you had against Mr. Richman?"

"The other charge is that he recently converted to Christianity,"

"Oh, really? How do you know this?"

"His wife mentioned it after she visited him. She was quite upset with the revelation and wanted us to know,"

"I would be too if someone in my family took leave of their senses and become one of those people. I'm not going to bother asking why you did it, Mr. Richman, I've already gone through the explanations a couple of times today and I don't want a bigger headache. So, we'll go straight to what your punishment will be." Boyd banged the gavel, indicating the next phase of the trial. "Tim Richman, you've been found guilty. Your punishment will be death, which is scheduled for tomorrow. Guards, escort him to the temporary cellblock for death penalty cases. Case dismissed." Boyd banged the gavel again. "Since it's close to five and near the end of this court's day, this court is dismissed for the day. We will reconvene again tomorrow morning at eight."

The crowd dispersed and the guards escorted Richman to the cellblock where the condemned prisoners were, and put him in with the five other Christians that had been on trial. Pastor Rogers approached and said, "We've been praying off and on for the past several hours. We're not praying for ourselves, but for our nation and for someone to witness to the lost before it's too late. I know you don't have much experience when it comes to praying, especially out loud, but would you like to join us?"

"Sure, I'd be honored."

The group prayed together. Later, the men shared how they ended up in jail. Pastor Rogers shared his story and then Tim told everyone how he ended up in jail due to his burning of buildings, then his meeting Rogers, and then coming to Christ.

After Richman and Rogers shared their stories, the next to share his story was fifty-five year old Lance Poston. "I coach, uh coached, high school football. For years, my teams and I have prayed before each game and many of my players came to Bible study. The school administrators and the district never seemed to have a problem with it, so they never said anything to me. Then, unexpectedly, a parent whose children weren't even in the school's athletics program, complained to anyone who would listen how I was destroying the kids' psyches and I was indoctrinating them. So, I was arrested and here I am,"

"It's irritating how some people think they can stick their noses into other people's business. Did your team and their parents stick up for you?" asked Rogers.

"No they didn't. I felt like they had stuck a knife in my back. I would've thought someone would've stuck up for my beliefs, but even the ones who I thought were believers kept their mouths shut. It's all very baffling, but I guess that's the times we live in."

The next to share was twenty-three year old David Shepherd. "I'm a college student at North Texas, and I was set to graduate next year. Anyway, one of my professors decided he didn't like people saying God bless you to anyone who sneezed or coughed during class, so he put that in his syllabus and said his word was law. A majority of the students obeyed his command, but I thought it was stupid, so I ignored it. For a while, he would knock off points on my research papers and tests each time I did it. But, one day he apparently decided he'd had enough, made an excuse to leave the classroom, and ten minutes later came back with a campus police officer. The professor demanded that the officer remove me, so the officer did as he was told. The university pressed charges against me and that's why I'm here,"

"Why didn't you just follow the class rules?" asked Richman.

"I don't know, I guess I felt like it was a stupid rule and I was offended that he was offended by God. Most of the time, professors don't even follow their own rules in the syllabus, so I didn't expect him to. Live and learn, I guess."

The last two men were going door-to-door in neighborhoods witnessing to people about Christ. The older of the two was forty-year-old Kyle Oakdale, and the younger was thirty-year-old Wayne Westwood. Kyle spoke, "Everything was going well that day. Of the houses we visited, five families wanted to know more, so we invited them to our church, and they said they'd go. Then, we came to the home of a Muslim family,"

"That's when events turned against us," Wayne added.

"The head of the family, a rather angry looking man, opened the door. I was about to say who we were when he saw we had our Bibles and noticed that we looked the part of Christian missionaries. He demanded we leave his property immediately, because he would not tolerate Christians in his presence. But, before we could even turn around to leave, one of the Burqa-clad females in his family handed him a cell phone because she had already called the police. He told the police that if they didn't come to arrest us, he and his fellow Muslims in the area would make a big stink on social media that they were being unfairly treated. If that didn't work, they'd call their lawyers and the Council for Muslim whatever, get the national media to side with them, and they even threatened to organize a riot to show how serious they were if they didn't get their way. So, the police came and arrested us,"

"You know, it's been said that once the Muslim population gets to twenty percent anywhere, they start demanding that everything and everyone bow to their will. I remember Dearborn, Michigan, being one of their early experiments in the United States. Turning the city completely Muslim was successful, so they made an effort to spread across the rest of the country to attempt to turn us the same way they turned Europe during the Syrian Civil War," said Rogers.

"I've heard that about them. My father was a missionary in Austria when that happened and he was one of the last to leave before the Muslims began systematically purging Europe of Christians who wouldn't recant and join Islam. I'm surprised the Roman Catholics still remain headquartered in Rome," replied Westwood.

"That's because the Pope wants to join all the world's religions together, but he views us literal Bible believing Christians as the enemy, which is part of Bible prophecy after all. I'm not going to worry about it, because God wins in the end. Now, let's all get some sleep, we have a big day ahead of us tomorrow." Rogers sarcastically said, as he laid down and closed his eyes. The others did the same.

Chapter 11

The next day, the men were woken up by the guards, one of whom said, "All right, sleepy heads, today's the big day. Get up do we can give you your last meal."

The last meal consisted of cold, lumpy oatmeal, barely drinkable orange juice, and hard toast with barely any butter lathered on the bread. Pastor Rogers asked one of the guards, "Do you mind if we pray over our meal?"

The man shrugged and replied, "Don't bother me none, your kind will be out of the way soon enough."

"Boy, that sounds like a ringing endorsement," Richman sarcastically observed.

"We take what we can get, Tim." replied Rogers. "Okay, let's go ahead and pray. Dear Heavenly Father, we come to you this day asking that you give us the strength and the wisdom to be able to handle our impending deaths. Help us not to be weak, but strong, in front of the many people who will be observing our executions. If it's possible, let how we handle our deaths be the impetus needed for others to come to you and get saved from their sins. I pray that our leaders see the evil they're doing before it's too late. I pray for our fellow man as the anti-Christ and the false prophet arrive on the world scene; please let those people not be deceived so that they end up in Hell. I thank you for saving me from my sins and I look forward to seeing you in Heaven when I die. Please bless the food we're about to eat. Thank you for everything you've done for us. In Jesus' name, I pray, amen."

The men barely had time to finish their meals when the guards came back, this time with shackles, to keep them from running or trying to attack the guards. The head guard said, "Now that we have all of you secured, we're going to take you to the bus to transport you to the execution site." The prisoners were in shackles five minutes later, so he said, "Let's go."

The condemned men were led into the garage, directed towards a white painted school bus with Texas Department of Corrections written on the side, and they were told to get in. Rogers asked, "Don't you guys usually transfer prisoners to a bus parked at the outside parking lot?"

"Yeah, but you guys aren't the usual prisoners. My superiors think this is safer, because who knows how many people out there are gunning to take you down before your public executions. The media only know the times of the executions, but they have no idea where we're coming from and in what kind of vehicle. Control of information is very important in this situation," said the guard.

"Oh, I see,"

"Stop asking questions and get in the bus."

"Yes, sir."

On the bus, the guards shackled the men to posts installed next to their seats, the thinking was that it would prevent prisoners from escaping, even if the bus was involved in a wreck. The bus started up a short time later, and they were off to wherever the executions would take place. The men discovered the day bright and sunny with not a cloud in the sky. Traffic was heavy as always on the interstate the bus traveled on, but none of the men could tell whether the national media had drones trailing the bus or even if the local media were following in their vehicles. As far as the condemned men could tell, no one on the interstate cared that a Texas Department of Corrections bus was on the same road. Overall, the trip was quiet.

The men were surprised when the bus stopped in the parking lot of the Cotton Bowl Stadium, on the grounds of the State Fair of Texas. The parking lot was full of cars, they could see the vehicles of the various media, and there were even souvenir trucks close to the entrances, which had lines of people waiting to buy something. The guards unlatched the shackles, led the men off the bus, and into the stadium.

No one seemed worried about the Ebola outbreak, because the men found themselves on the field, where they could see that the stadium was completely full, no seat empty. The people in the stands gave off the impression that they were in a celebratory mood and the men were shocked that so many were so easily led into being bloodthirsty. Rogers thought, *I wonder if this is how the Romans acted when they were putting people to death in the Coliseum all those centuries ago?*

At the fifty-yard line, a sort of gallows was set up, but instead of ropes for hanging, it looked like old-fashioned wooden blocks where a person would kneel down and place their head on it had been placed. Large men, who were head to toe in black, including a black covering over their faces, held large axes in their hands, and were waiting for the orders to behead someone. Rogers noticed a communications device, probably an intercom, near one of the executioners, and he wondered if the orders to execute he and the others would come from whoever was on the other end of that device.

Kyle Oakdale muttered, “What? No guillotine? I’m disappointed.”

“They probably thought a guillotine wasn’t intimidating enough and not very personal,” Rogers whispered back.

“Those guys who are about to behead us, must have some kind of blood lust, or are just flat-out psychotic, and that goes the same for the crowd. What are they chanting?” asked Richman.

“I think they’re chanting ‘Off with their heads!’ and maybe a bit of ‘Crucify them!’ It’s giving me goosebumps and not in a good way,” replied Wayne Westwood, who flinched as he would if he suddenly felt cold.

“Do you think we’re in the Tribulation?” asked David Shepherd.

“No, I don’t think so, but we are probably days or months from the beginnings of it. Once we true Christians are out of the way, the anti-Christ should be revealed to the world,” replied Rogers.

“Do you have any ideas on who it could be?

“I have no idea, but I do think the false prophet is that new Pope, he’ll probably introduce the anti-Christ to the world.” Rogers replied and then the men fell silent.

As they were led to the gallows, a camera crew could be seen filming on the structure, while drones buzzed in the sky above the stadium, also filming the action that was about to take place. Rogers was the first to step onto the gallows, when a microphone was suddenly thrust in front of him, and camera lights almost blinded him. "What? What's going on?" he asked.

The reporter, or so Rogers thought, looked vaguely Arabic to Rogers, making him wonder if the men with the axes were Muslims. The man said, "Ladies and gentlemen, at home and here in the stadium, I present you Pastor Sam Rogers, who has been condemned to die for his crimes against the State." A chorus of boos rained down from the stands. "Before he dies, I will ask him the same question I've asked all of our condemned - will he recant his beliefs and join us. So, Pastor Rogers, do you recant? Will you say you'll join the world community in condemning beliefs that are considered detrimental to your fellow man?"

"No, I won't. I believe Jesus died for my sins and saved me so I can go to Heaven. He will do the same for all of you who repent, before it is too late to do anything about it. I reject your new world order and the coming world leader who will destroy everything to get what he wants. I accept my fate, so whatever you do to my body doesn't matter, for I know where my soul will be when I die."

"There you have it, ladies and gentlemen, an unrepentant criminal. I'm sure if I asked his five friends the same question, I'd get the same pathetic answer, so I won't anger you all with their answers. Are you ready for their beheadings?"

The crowd shook the stadium by answering loudly in the affirmative and they cheered when the men were led to the blocks, where they were forced to lay down, with their necks exposed. A buzzing sound suddenly came from the communications device. If Rogers and the others were able to see it, they would've seen a green light activate, which indicated their beheadings could start at any time.

"Executioners, begin!" shouted the man with the microphone.

The executioners raised their axes high in the air and swung with all their might into the necks of the condemned Christian men. The heads easily separated from the bodies and fell into the baskets that were there to catch the heads. Other men appeared on stage and collected the headless bodies, presumably to bury them somewhere. The crowd's cheers were deafening as they celebrated the beheadings and the ratings on television were high for that time of day.

The powers-that-be were pleased with the results and decided they would plan more of these public beheadings as soon as they could find more of the true believers, wherever they were hiding.

Chapter 12

Meanwhile, Doctor Kirkland had no idea any of this was going on. He was working at the hospital on his usual rounds with no idea what was happening in the outside world. Right now, his biggest concern was the unusual Ebola cases coming into the hospital. The people coming in were showing signs of the virus, but the virus itself wasn't acting the way it traditionally did, mostly because these patients weren't dying horrible deaths, just had prolonged pain and wished to be dead.

"Nurse Frye, I'm going to do a blood test on one of our infected patients, so I can see what's going on in the bloodstream. Will you please assist me?"

"Okay, Doctor, but have you taken all the precautions first?" asked the soon-to-retire nurse.

"Of course I have. I don't want to be the first medical professional in over fifteen years to be diagnosed with Ebola and then end up causing problems for the hospital administrators. Ready?"

"As ready as I'll ever be, Doctor."

"All right, let's go."

The two entered the room of a male Ebola patient in his fifties who had been constantly throwing up and blood usually issued from his ears, eyes, mouth, and nose. The man should've been dead weeks ago, but he definitely wasn't, which was why Kirkland decided to do some bloodwork so he could find out why. Most of the time, the man was unconscious because the nursing staff kept him drugged so he wouldn't be awake and in constant pain, and this time was no different.

Nurse Frye prepared the man's arm for the syringe needle that would go into his bicep. Kirkland prepared the syringe, carefully inserted the needle into the man's right bicep after Frye finished, and withdrew the blood he needed. The nurse cleaned the area around the bicep, made sure the patient was comfortable, checked his IV's to make sure they were full of the medicines and nutrients he needed, and then she left the room while Doctor Kirkland headed for the lab.

In the lab, Kirkland took a sample from the blood and placed it under the lens of the most powerful microscope the hospital owned so he could figure out what was going on with the blood chemistry. He realized he should've done this weeks ago, especially since Overseer Dodd was upset the hospital had many patients that were sucking the government dry because they continued to live beyond what Dodd thought they ought to live. Kirkland constantly prayed that he could somehow lead Dodd to the Lord, but so far, he hadn't found an appropriate opening to ask her about her soul and where it would be when she died.

Looking into the microscope, Kirkland adjusted it so he could see the individual red and white blood cells in the sample. He wasn't at all prepared for what he saw, it was like something out of a science fiction movie. From his point of view, he thought they were little robots that were infecting the blood. Some of them looked damaged, while others apparently weren't functioning, but there were hundreds of others still working to destroy the blood cells with what looked like the Ebola virus. Kirkland thought, *This is above my head, maybe I ought to consult with Dodd. Hopefully, others have noticed this and reported these tiny robots in the bloodstream of all these patients. If others have noticed, there could be a solution to get rid of the robots.* Kirkland paged Dodd to come to the lab.

A few minutes later, she came in, and rudely asked, "What do you want?"

"I took a look at the blood of one our Ebola patients, what I found was not what I expected,"

"What do you mean?"

"Well, take a look for yourself,"

Dodd went over to the microscope to look and saw the nanobots that infected the blood. She wasn't at all surprised, because she knew about the project the people above her had started. She knew that the goal for these nanobots was to kill off at least a billion people, but that hadn't happened, because only half a billion had died across the planet. She wasn't sure what to do about Kirkland discovering this, other than consulting with her superiors about what to do next.

She stood up straight to face Kirkland, tried to look concerned, and said, "I'll have to inform my superiors about this and find out if other doctors have discovered these so-called robots in other peoples' bloodstreams. If someone has found a way to counteract this problem, I'm sure they'll know about it. In the meantime, continue making your rounds and I'll get back to you later, Okay?"

Kirkland suspected Dodd knew something, and maybe was lying about it, but said, "All right, I'll visit my other patients while you consult with your superiors. Thanks for coming down to look."

"Sure, no problem." Dodd left the room and headed for her office.

Once in her office, she activated the webcam on her computer, sent the person she needed to talk to an instant message, and she waited for the person's appearance. Dodd waited for fifteen minutes before the man appeared on her screen, it was Joseph Barker, who asked, "How can I help you, Miss Dodd?"

"I think we have a problem. One of the doctors in this hospital discovered the nanobots in the blood of one of the infected patients. He's also pointed out they seem to be malfunctioning,"

"Yes, this doctor of yours could be a problem. As for the nanobots malfunctioning, that's a problem we discovered weeks ago from some other doctors who had access to labs, and we've discovered that it's a problem in their programming. Since the nanobots are copies of copies of the few dozen that we started with, the programming has decayed, causing malfunctions. However, enough people have died from the results for the malfunctions not to matter all that much. Do you think the doctor would keep quiet if you told him what was really going on?"

"I don't think so. He seems like one of those upright types who will always do the right thing, no matter what,"

"I see. Before we do anything, find out where he would stand on this issue, whether he's with us or against us. Most of the doctors who discovered the nanobots have been with us. If he's against us, especially in every way possible, we'll take care of the problem. Is he still at work?"

"Yes, sir,"

Okay, go find out where he stands while he's still there. Contact me again when you find out."

"I'll do that, sir."

Barker signed off, while Dodd went to look for Kirkland. She didn't feel comfortable paging him over the intercom, because doing so would let the entire hospital know she would be speaking to him. If Kirkland suddenly disappeared whether now or later, too many people would know Dodd was the last to see him, and she couldn't let that happen.

Dodd found Kirkland in the hallway going to see his next patient. She stopped him and said, "I need to speak to you, in private,"

"You spoke with your superiors?"

"Yes, that's why I need to speak to you in private. Let's go to your office, since it's closer. Okay?"

Although suspicious of her motives, he agreed, "All right, let's go."

Once in Kirkland's office, the doctor sat down in his chair and motioned for Dodd to sit in the guest chair. When she sat down, he asked, "So, what did you find out?"

Taking a deep breath, she began, "What I'm about to tell you is classified, you can't tell anyone, and if you do tell anyone, my superiors will do what they have to do to keep you silent. Understood?"

"Yes,"

"All right, good. So the nanobots you discovered are a secret initiative to lower the population of Earth to make it more sustainable for the rest of us to live here. With a lower population, we can lower greenhouse gasses to prevent climate change, stop the polar ice caps from melting, and make everyone use sustainable energy, like solar and wind power. This is something the people of this planet cannot know about; otherwise, we'd have major problems, like rioting, for instance,"

Kirkland wasn't sure what to say, but he knew what Dodd revealed was bad for the people of Earth. His thoughts came to the idea that it was probably part of the end times era that Pastor Rogers had talked about on Sunday's. The end times and whatever came from that was something Kirkland couldn't do anything about, since it was God's plan to eventually purge the Earth of all sin. He needed answers from Dodd.

"So you're saying that Christians are being persecuted to further the agenda of those who want fewer people on Earth and a one world government?"

"Yes,"

"Can I ask why?"

"Well, because those people who consider themselves true believers or whatever you want to call them, are against those of us who want everyone to worship the same way and to bow their knee to one government, instead of many governments – from local to state to federal. Blaming those true believers for a virus is easy. Many of the un-thinking people on this planet will believe they did it and demand something, anything, be done to rid the planet of them. As we speak, that problem is being taken care of,"

"What do you mean?" Kirkland decided he didn't like where this conversation was headed.

"Concerned citizens have been rounding up the so-called true believers, some are put on trial, and all of them are executed. But, really, there's no need to concern yourself with any of that, because all my superiors want to know is if you would keep this to yourself and if you would cooperate with us by not letting the whole world know,"

Kirkland wondered if the so-called concerned citizens rounded up his new church family. If they had, he also wondered if there was anything he could do for them. Doing his best to remain calm and unattached, he replied, "You know, I'll have to think about it. What would happen to me if I didn't want to cooperate, but kept my mouth shut all the same?"

"Bad things could happen to you, Doctor, if you didn't cooperate, so if you need the time to think about it, I'll give one day and that's all. No matter what you do, if you decide on the wrong answer or even decide to cooperate, I'll have to inform my superiors. What they do after your decision is entirely their purview, I don't make those decisions. Do you understand?"

"Perfectly, Miss Dodd,"

"Good. All right, you have exactly one day to make your choice. We'll meet here, in your office, in exactly twenty-four hours. If you need to go home now to think, you have permission,"

"Okay, I'll do that."

"I look forward to your decision. See you tomorrow." Dodd walked out of the office, much to Kirkland's relief, since he felt a lot of evil emanating from her and it made him uncomfortable. Dodd informed Barker that Kirkland would have a decision for them in twenty-four hours.

Kirkland left the building and began praying while he walked through the parking garage to his car, *Heavenly Father, I don't know much about end times prophecy, so please help me in these dangerous times. I pray for my friends at church. If they're in trouble, please protect them and let them know you're still in charge. I ask that you give them the strength and wisdom to deal with whatever is happening in their lives. Thank you again for coming into my life. In your name, amen.*

Instead of going home, Kirkland drove to the Rogers home to see if they were safe and if they had an idea of what was going on. Before he even got to the property, Kirkland could see some smoke coming from where the house was supposed to be, and it worried him. Driving onto the property, he saw the now smoking ruins of the Rogers home, with the cars of the congregation still parked. He stopped his car and parked it so he could get out and look around.

Kirkland didn't have to go very far before he found the headless bodies, which would've sickened him if he wasn't a doctor and hadn't seen all sorts of gruesome sights while working in the hospital for his entire career so far. Unfortunately, what did shock him was the sight of the heads of the people stuck on fence posts along the fence line. He thought that whoever had done the foul deed had a very malicious and hateful heart. Kirkland unhappily looked at each one and eventually discovered that Pastor Rogers was not one of the beheaded people. *I wonder what happened to the pastor? I wonder if I should call the authorities? What should I do now? Lord, please guide me to the right decision.*

Chapter 13

Feeling overwhelmed by the discovery of his dead friends, Kirkland dropped to his knees and cried. Although he knew they were in Heaven, he suddenly felt very alone, and he wasn't entirely sure what to do about it. After he stopped crying, he finally decided he should probably bury the dead, no matter how gruesome it would be to remove the detached heads from fence posts, but it had to be done. The barn still stood, so Kirkland headed for it, to see what kind of machinery he could find so he didn't have to spend days using just a shovel to bury over fifty people.

In the barn, Kirkland found a Bobcat with a backhoe attachment, alongside a much bigger Caterpillar with the backhoe and its other, much bigger accessories off to the side. He figured it would be easier to fit the backhoe attachment to the Bobcat, even though he was a doctor, not a mechanic. After finding some gloves to protect his hands, Kirkland got to work. Thirty minutes later, and completely covered in oil and grime, the doctor managed to get the backhoe attached to the Bobcat. He got into the cab, started it up, drove the Bobcat out of the barn out to where the bodies were lying, and began digging out individual graves for his brothers and sisters in Christ.

Hours later, Kirkland finished burying the dead, so he put the equipment back up, even though it really wasn't necessary now that no one lived here. He knew he needed to go home to get out his blood and grime covered clothes, and probably get some sleep due to how exhausted he felt, but beyond that, he wasn't sure what to do. He didn't think going back to work was a good idea, because who knew what bad things Dodd and her friends would do to him when they found out he wouldn't be playing along with their scheme. *Lord, please give me a hint or something!*

Before he could do anything, a brown Suburban pulled into the driveway. Kirkland was relieved to see that the vehicle had regular license plates and not United States government plates, but he still wondered if he should get into his car and drive away as quickly as possible. All sorts of scenarios played out in his mind as the six people inside stepped out of the SUV.

The first to speak was an older man, who had the bearing of someone who was once in the military, and had some sort of authority while in the service, "Excuse me, is this the home of Pastor Samuel Rogers?"

"Yes, at least it was. I think he ended up in prison, but I don't know for sure. His congregation ended up beheaded and I just finished burying the bodies,"

The new arrivals had shocked looks on their faces, but the older man said, "I had hoped to get here before they killed Rogers and his congregation. I guess we were too late. How were you spared?"

"I was at work when this happened. I'm a doctor at one of the more advanced hospitals in the area. My name is Neal Kirkland,"

The two shook hands, "I see. Well, it's good to meet you, Doctor Kirkland, I'm Colonel Jason Turner of the U.S. Air Force. These five with me are fellow Christians from various units under my command. We managed to get away before they purged what was left of the military of the very few Christians still in the service. We ditched our uniforms and anything they could use to track us before heading off to see Rogers. The pastor was an old friend of mine; we served together during the war in Iraq all those years ago,"

"Really? What did you do?"

"We were in the cyber warfare division. You know, a country hacks your computers, so you return the favor, or you plant a virus in your enemy's computers so they won't have the ability to know what's going with your troop movements,"

"Oh, I see. So none of you were in the position to push back against the government when they took away civilian guns and restricted more of our freedoms?"

"Believe me, some of us tried to warn the public, but we were limited by our superiors, some of whom were political appointees and were more interested in pleasing the President. As for the guns, we also tried warning the more conservative online media about all the false flag attacks at schools and colleges,"

"Were all those mass shootings faked?" interrupted Kirkland, who was shocked to hear the Colonel imply they were.

"Not all of them, only that first one at that elementary school in New England. That one was supposed to be about testing reaction times from first responders and the community. Unfortunately, the media grabbed a hold of it and turned it into something it was not. The federal government followed along so they could push their anti-gun agenda and also convinced the community to go along with the scheme. Government agents and jihadists that were part of the cause carried out the rest of the shootings. Mass killings continued nearly every month for the next six months until the President and Congress finally convinced the American people that gun confiscation needed to happen, and it did because the American people submitted like the sheep they are,"

"You knew this and did nothing?" Kirkland felt his anger rising.

"I didn't know anything about this at the time. I learned about all of this before I decided to go AWOL. I accessed the government's database and found a lot of this information by accident. I was looking for other information that I could take to the mainstream media to warn the people that their government was going beyond what they were supposed to do according to the Constitution. I found one thread and then another, and before I knew it, I'd gone down the rabbit hole, where I found out what I just told you. I'm sure others would have informed the public, but according to the information I read, the FCC had threatened to withdraw licenses from the media if they had told anyone, so the stories got buried. Because I felt like the government was looking over my shoulder because of my relationship with Christ, I decided that I needed to do something, so I thought Rogers might help me,"

"I understand now. I've got the government looking over my shoulder every minute of the day, including putting me in a position where I've got one particular problem that I'm not sure how to deal with,"

Curious about Kirkland's problem, Turner asked, "Is it anything we can help you with?"

"I don't know, but I don't suppose it would hurt to tell you about it. Well, to make a long story short, I discovered through some bloodwork that the Ebola virus is artificial, maintained by nanobots, and I think our government is involved,"

"An artificial virus being created to kill people doesn't surprise me, given how wicked people have become in the last few decades. What happened next?"

"When I learned about it, my superior gave me twenty-four hours to decide whether I would help them keep it a secret. If I don't, I'm sure I'm dead. Is there a way you could help me?"

"We might be able to. Do you have the information with you so we can try to alert the media?"

"No, but I could go back to the hospital and gather the information. I could probably get into the office of the government agent in charge of our hospital and access her computer,"

"Wouldn't you be caught?"

"No, the overseer goes home each day at five, and it's now long past that. The hospital staff wouldn't blink an eye if they saw me come in, since I sometimes work various shifts. I can get into her office, access her computer, download whatever information I need into a flash drive, and then leave. I'll even retrieve the results of the bloodwork, if that would help,"

"I think you have a solid plan, but I think we should go with you, so you'll have an extra set of eyes looking out for trouble. We might not have time to retrieve the bloodwork, so expect to only retrieve the data,"

"Okay, I understand. Now what do we do next?"

"Well, now the next thing you ought to do is go home and get cleaned up,"

Looking down at his soiled clothes, Kirkland had forgotten how awful he must look to the six people in front of him. Slightly embarrassed, he replied, "Oh, right. Okay, follow me home and we'll go from there." He got into his car and led the way to his home.

On the way home, Kirkland thanked God that He answered the doctor's prayers about what he should do next. Although a part of him was wary of the motives of Turner and his people, the doctor decided to trust in God. Even though going back to the hospital seemed very risky, Kirkland knew God was behind him all the way.

Chapter 14

Arriving at Kirkland's house, they found that it was a mansion in Preston Hollow, close to University Park, where many of Dallas' rich and famous lived, including a former President of the United States. The mansion was five thousand square feet, had four bathrooms and six bedrooms, with a pool in the backyard, and a four-car garage. Turner said, "You have a nice home,"

"Thank you, but it's too big for me though. Unfortunately, I don't really have time to sell it. This mansion was for my wife when she was alive, because she loved to throw parties, and my income was such that we could afford it. We have four children, but they're gone and are living their own lives, so I no longer need something so lavish,"

"I'm sorry, Doctor,"

"Oh, no worries and please call me Neal,"

"Okay, Neal,"

"All right, please make yourselves at home while I take a shower and get into some clean clothes. The fridge is full and the TV's connected to every streaming video service currently available, but I do have satellite if you prefer to watch the news or whatever,"

"Thanks, Neal." replied Turner.

"No problem." Kirkland headed for his bedroom, thinking, *I wish we had time to let me get some sleep, maybe three or four hours' worth, but we have work to do, and the sooner it gets done, the better off we'll be. Maybe getting into the shower will wake me up.*

Turner turned on the television to cable news because he wanted to find out what was going on in the world. The five younger officers went to the kitchen to find something to eat. Turner stopped at one news network when he saw they would have a report coming up about Christian executions.

The news anchor began, "If you missed the live broadcast from earlier today, we have the highlights from the executions of Christians carried out around the country. If you'd like to see the full videos, please visit our website where all videos are posted. Now, here are highlights from around the country,"

Turner watched in morbid fascination as the news showed the names of the condemned, all of them were Christian, and then their beheadings. When the name of Sam Rogers and the video highlight of his execution appeared on the screen, Turner wasn't at all surprised, even though it saddened him that his friend was tried, convicted, and then beheaded all for being a Christian. Turner took solace in the fact he would see Rogers and the other martyrs in Heaven later. The other five returned from the kitchen and set down some food that was on a serving tray onto the coffee table. Turner took a peanut butter sandwich and a Coke from the tray and they watched the rest of the news together.

The highlights ended and the anchor reappeared, saying, "In other news, Israel has decided to destroy the Muslim mosque known as the Dome of the Rock. They claim the leaders of the mosque promote violence against the Jews, especially against those worshipping at the Western Wall. Israel's leaders also wanted the Dome of the Rock gone because they're about to rebuild their own temple. They claim the building's blueprints are finished, the contractor and his staff are prepared for the next stage, and all that's needed is to clear the land before the real work begins. With this proclamation from Israel, the Muslim leadership, from Iran to Germany to the United States, has asked the United Nations to sanction and boycott the Jews. Some even want military action from Iran or Russia, who took over

Syria years ago, to invade Israel to prevent them from destroying the Dome of the Rock. Whatever happens, we will continue to follow the story and will break in to programming when necessary. Our other major story for tonight is about….."

Turner decided to change the channel when the anchor was in mid-sentence, while saying to the others, "So, it's begun,"

"What's begun?" asked Kirkland as he walked into the living room, looking less weary than he had when he came home.

"I think we're coming closer to the Rapture,"

"Really? How do you know this?"

"Well, because Israel is going to rebuild their temple, and that'll only happen during the Tribulation Period. In order for the Tribulation Period to happen, which I'm sure Rogers preached about, the church has to be removed from Earth,"

"He did and I'm looking forward to whenever the Rapture happens. Did you learn anything else from the news? Like, anything about Ebola?"

"No, but I did see a video highlight of Christians being executed, including Rogers. You can go to that cable stations' website to take a look if you want to, but it would be very disturbing and heart wrenching,"

"No, that's all right, I can do without seeing someone beheaded. I just wish there was something we could've done to prevent their murders and I'm sorry we couldn't help Pastor Rogers, his family, the congregation, and other fellow Christians in their times of need. At least they're in Heaven with Christ and don't have to suffer here on Earth any longer,"

"That's true, Doctor. You know, sometimes I wish our Christian ancestors hadn't thought politics was beneath them, because our country would not be in the position it is now. Unfortunately, we can't change that and neither can we change the unjust way our brothers and sisters in Christ are currently being treated. Now then, are you ready to go back to the hospital to retrieve the data?"

"Yes, but once we get the data, don't you think we should avoid coming back here? Once I don't show up at the pre-requisite time to tell my superior my decision, they'll come looking for me, and this is the first place they'll look,"

"I had planned on not coming back here anyway, so need to worry about that. We can alert the media about our discovery from anywhere as long as we have a stable internet connection. I have an idea where to go, and that's to my cabin at Lake Texoma,"

"Great. All right, before we go, I think we ought to pray. Colonel, would you lead it?"

"Okay. Heavenly Father, we ask for traveling mercies on the interstate as we go back to Doctor Kirkland's hospital to get the data. We ask that we're protected from the forces of evil while we're at the hospital. Once we get the data, please guide us and help us to have the wisdom to do what's needed. Thank you for dying for our sins and being our Lord and Savior. Thank you for everything you do for us, in your name, I pray, amen."

Yawning, Kirkland said, "Okay, let's get going."

Chapter 15

At the hospital, even though it was three in the morning, it was just as busy as it was during the day because of all the Ebola patients the hospital cared for. Turner had his people watch the hospital's entrances for any military or police response in case Kirkland's access of Dodd's computer activated some kind of alarm. They each had communications devices so they could warn each other if someone in authority was coming into the hospital. At Dodd's office door, no one noticed the two men when they slipped into her office.

"First off, I need to see if her computer's password protected. Because if it is, I don't think I'd be able to get in," stated Kirkland.

"Don't you worry about that, I have a device that can run through thousands of passwords a minute. From my experience, people like Dodd tend to have fairly simple, straightforward passwords that are easy to remember,"

Kirkland shrugged, replying, "If you say so." The he sat in Dodd's chair, played with the computer mouse to see if the computer was still running instead of asleep or shutdown altogether. The monitor had gone dark because it was in power saving mode. Kirkland saw that it went instantly to the desktop because there was no password protection. “Great, this should be easy, and as far as I can tell, we haven’t activated some kind of alarm. Now to search for the Ebola files,”

Kirkland went to the search button on the start menu of the latest version of the Windows software and typed in “Ebola” so he could see what listed files showed up that were on this computer. He found there was only one, it was the main folder, but it had dozens of subfolders in the directory. Kirkland inserted the flash drive into the USB access point in the desktop and then copied the whole folder to the flash drive. However, before he got up from the desk chair, Kirkland decided to look at the folder, because his curiosity was getting the better of him.

“Let’s see what we have here,” he muttered.

“What are you doing?” asked an obviously impatient Turner.

“I’m just checking out these files to see what’s really been going on,”

“We really don’t have the time, Doctor. If someone discovers us, we’ll be in big trouble. You can take a look at those files at my cabin, all right?”

"All right, fine. Let's get out of here before anyone sees us and questions why we're in Dodd's office. Do you think we have time to go to the lab to retrieve the bloodwork?"

"No, what we're doing is risky enough. Come on, let's go."

Kirkland got out of the chair and both men left the office, doing their best to remain unseen by the busy hospital staff. In the parking lot, the other five joined them after Turner contacted them and told them to return to the vehicle. They got into the Suburban and headed for Lake Texoma.

Meanwhile, Gina Dodd was sound asleep in her bed when her cell phone rang, startling her out of her sleep. Although very groggy, the ringtone from the call indicated to her that someone much higher in power than herself was calling her. She touched the screen, not really seeing the Caller ID, and set it to where she could hear whoever it was without placing the phone next to her ear. "Hello? Who is this?"

"Miss Dodd, your computer and the file we've had on watch has been accessed,"

"What file? Who is this?" she asked, still groggy.

She heard the man sigh, and then he replied with some exasperation in his voice, "We're not on a secured line, so I'm not telling you who I am, at least not until you get to your office so we can speak face-to-face via the way we always communicate with each other. If you'd wake up, you'll remember which file I'm referring to. So, get out of bed, get dressed, and get to your office as soon as you can. Do you understand your orders?"

"Yeah, yeah, I understand. I'll be there in about an hour,"

"Fine. Goodbye." The call ended.

"Whatever. I don't get paid enough for this crap." Dodd angrily muttered as she set the phone down and began getting ready to go to work.

When she arrived at the hospital, Dodd went directly to her office without speaking to any of the staff. Sitting down at her desk, Dodd secured the channel they would speak on, and then let the man know that she was ready to speak with him. She turned on her webcam and waited until the man showed up.

The richest man on Earth's face popped up on screen five minutes later, and he said, "Good morning, Miss Dodd,"

Grumpily, she replied, "Good morning, Mr. Morris. So, what was so important that you had to get me out of bed?"

"Now, now, no need to be grumpy,"

She rolled her eyes. "Yes, sir. All right, what's going on?"

"About two hours ago, your computer was accessed and the Ebola file was downloaded,"

"Oh no. Do you know who did it?"

"Yes, I do. Hospital cameras recorded Doctor Kirkland and a man I didn't recognize sneaking into your office. I expected Kirkland to pull a stunt like this, considering what you told him yesterday,"

Panicking, Dodd replied, "But what about the Ebola files? Those files contain everything about who created it and why. We're in big trouble if he goes to the authorities or even the media,"

"There's no need to worry, the files he took were not the real ones. One of my associates planted fake information that will implicate the United States government and military. If the information gets distributed the way we think it will, the United States will no longer be a hindrance to our plans. The appropriate parties will take action against the United States as a response to the Ebola virus. In that case, I suggest you leave the Metroplex,"

"What'll happen?"

"Major American cities, with the exception of New York, will be hit with nuclear weapons. I'm sure you don't want to be caught in a nuclear explosion,"

"Of course I don't. When will it happen?"

"Oh, probably within a day, or even up to a week after the Ebola story being reported on the news. Various countries, like Russia or China, have to pretend to be seriously concerned, and then they'll take action. I suggest you not stay in the city too long after the story ends up on the news,"

"I won't. What are you going to do about Doctor Kirkland?"

"We sent a team out to his house, but he wasn't there. We'll figure out where he is when he sends the data to various news organizations,"

"Will any of the mainstream media outlets cooperate, since they're supposed to keep a lid on the real news?"

"They've been told to expect the information any minute and they'll do as they're told or risk being heavily fined,"

"Okay, do you need anything else from me before I go home and pack as much as I can?"

"I believe that's all I have to speak to you about. When you manage to get away from the Metroplex and have settled into a home somewhere else, you know how to contact us. Good luck, Miss Dodd."

“Thank you, Mr. Morris.” The screen went black when Morris cut the connection and Dodd said to herself, “Well, I guess I should go home and pack my clothes. I wonder where I should go?” She shrugged, then got up from her chair, walked out of her office for the last time, and headed home, not at all sure what she would do or where she would go once she left her house for the last time.

Chapter 16

At the cabin a few hours later, which was still early in the morning because the sun was still rising in the east, Turner uploaded the whole file into an email and sent it off to a variety of news outlets. Turner then said to everyone, "Now, we'll see if they take the bait and report on it or it'll go down the memory hole like most of the stories involving the government and we'll not hear about it - ever."

"I'm going to look through these files after I get some sleep," replied Kirkland.

"Go right ahead, Neal, you've probably been awake for more than a day, right?"

"Almost three days and I'm exhausted."

"We'll be here when you wake up. Sleep well."

"Thanks. Good night or good morning, whichever you prefer." Kirkland went back to one of the bedrooms and fell asleep the second he laid his head down on the pillow.

Events moved quickly once the media had the files. To Turner's surprise, the mainstream media began reporting on the newly found Ebola files on their noon broadcasts. He found the timing suspicious, but couldn't do anything about it, and he wasn't sure if he wanted to. The media claimed the virus to be genetically altered, instead of a synthetic creation and spread by nanotechnology. The virus, according to the media, was commissioned by the United States government and the military, then used Christian terrorists to spread it, even though none of it was really what the files said. The files hadn't mentioned Christians at all. Turner thought, *I wonder if Kirkland might've been manipulated into taking the files and we made a mistake not retrieving the blood samples. Oh well, hindsight is twenty/twenty after all. I wonder how this will turn out?*

Barely two hours had passed before Russia and China made known their views. In what seemed like a hastily assembled press conference, both of their United Nations ambassadors stood together, which was highly unusual for the two nations who were sometimes at odds. The Russian ambassador would be speaking for both of them.

"Good afternoon. Today we learned the United States, its military, and bioterrorists who align themselves with the Christian church were the ones responsible for the massive Ebola outbreak that killed nearly a billion people. We are outraged by this development. Because of the virus, the world economy is destabilizing and we place the blame squarely on the United States. We are calling on the United Nations to do something, even if China and Russia end up taking it upon ourselves to rectify the situation.

"For a long time, the United States has dictated to the rest of the world what they must do, but no one has ever had the strength to stand up to the United States and tell them to mind their own business. We plan to put an end to that, no matter what our colleagues in this building decide. The United States must pay for its crimes against humanity and we will do whatever it takes to make them pay. We will let you know what happens. Good day." Both ambassadors stepped away from the podium, taking no questions from the press.

Less than an hour later, the President of the United States appeared on television. Turner thought, *This whole thing with the virus and country's like Russia being outrageously outraged must be some kind of a scam. I wonder if the President is in on it? I don't think I'd be surprised at all if he was. Dear Lord in Heaven, please come quickly!*

The President sat behind his desk in the Oval Office, attempting to look serious because the situation was so serious. He began, "Good afternoon, my fellow

Americans. By now, you must've heard about the reports that the United States government and the military are involved with the Christian terrorists who unleashed the Ebola virus on the world. I'm here to tell you that it's simply not true, the federal government has no involvement in the outbreak or with the Christian terrorists and I will continue to deny it as long as I live.

"You've also heard that Russia and China have threatened the United States with some kind of action against us, probably military, if the United Nations doesn't do something. I warn both Russia and China that if they attempt anything, we will respond with equal force, or hit back harder, with nuclear weapons if necessary, to show them they don't mess with the United States. I ask my fellow Americans to stand with me against these threats and we will win as we always have when faced with dire situations. That's all I have to say, good night my fellow Americans."

The seal of the President of the United States showed on screen, ending the broadcast from the White House. The news anchors on the station that Turner and the five watched came on to summarize the day's events and to paraphrase what the President said in his speech. The talking heads said they had no idea what would happen next, but they would break into regular programming when something happened.

Doctor Kirkland finally came out of the bedroom, almost twelve hours after he went to sleep. To Turner, Kirkland looked rested, and the doctor asked, "I'm hungry; I think I'll eat something before I take a look at those files. So, have I missed anything?"

Turner was about to say something when all of them heard a trumpet call as clearly as they could hear each other, and they heard a voice say, "Come up hither!" In a twinkling of an eye, every saved by grace believer in Christ on Earth that were still among the living – disappeared. Since there were so few left, not many noticed, but that would change since God's hand of protection was withdrawn from the planet. Now the humans of Earth would experience something none of them had ever experienced before, and not a person would be spared from the coming judgments.

With the Christians gone, it took less than a day before Russia and China went ahead with their plans without any kind of sanctions or boycotts authorized by the United Nations. The first thing they did was detonate nukes high above the United States, causing an electromagnetic pulse that wiped out the electrical grid and anything powered with technology. The next action was to nuke the largest American cities and activate strategically placed nukes in the American west.

Gina Dodd was only as far as Parker County, west of Tarrant County, when the power in her car failed. The car slowed to halt on a hill that it was on and she got out of the car, not knowing what was wrong with it. In the corner of her eye, she saw a flash of bright light coming from the east, so she turned to see what it was. Even though she knew what was supposed to happen, Dodd was still shocked to see a mushroom cloud forming above Fort Worth, and she thought she could see the one over Dallas, even though that was over fifty miles away. The skyscrapers in downtown Fort Worth were no longer visible. Dodd wasn't sure if they had fallen, vaporized, or if dust clouds were just covering up her view. She could see a shockwave, but it was too far from her to affect her. Before she could do or think of anything, she felt an overwhelming darkness descend on her. Without thinking, the darkness guided her hand as she took out the handgun that was in the car's glovebox. Dodd raised the gun to her head and pulled the trigger, forever dooming her to an eternity in Hell.

The rest of the story to be continued in book two when the Anti-Christ rises and the Tribulation begins.

If you enjoyed this novel, then please leave a review on Amazon and please let your friends, family, co-workers, etc. know about this novel. Thanks!

In the meantime, check out Cliff's first end times series, The End Times Saga, which consists of seven novels and two short stories. If you prefer a box set, which is only the seven novels, it is available at various ebook retailers.

Please visit cliffball.net for more information about Cliff's novels, read short stories that are on the site, read the blog, and sign-up to get updates by e-mail about giveaways, sales, and future releases.

Other Works by Cliff Ball
Out of Time – time travel
The Usurper – political thriller
Beyond the New Frontier – alternate history
Dust Storm – Christian western short story
Voyager and the Aliens – sci-fi short story
An American Journey Series - Christian Historical Fiction
The Long Journey Book 1
and
The End Times Saga – Christian fiction:
Times of Turmoil
Times of Trouble
Times of Trial
Times of Rebellion
Times of Destruction
Times of Judgment
Times of Tribulation
Jon Ryan (short story)
Xavier Doolittle (short story)

Made in United States
North Haven, CT
18 September 2023

41699932R00107